Death at the Thistle Inn

Veronica Vale Investigates - book 10

Kitty Kildare

K.E. O'Connor Books

ISBN: 978-1-918248-03-6

DEATH AT THE THISTLE INN

Chapter 1

"Benji! You don't know these grounds. We must get inside the castle." My sturdy boots crunched over frozen bracken and through several inches of fresh snow as I searched for my overexcited dog.

Benji loved to explore new places, and the impressive grounds of Augustine Castle, near Loch Lomond, would be thrilling for him, with all the new scents and sights.

I was excited to be here, too. Escaping London was a rare treat, but we weren't hiking and discovering new places today, no matter how breathtaking the surroundings.

A startled bark rang out, and I increased my pace, glad of my practical flat-soled boots and my new thick, woollen winter coat. Neither was the height of fashion, but the coat was gloriously warm, and I could confidently walk for hours in these boots. What people said about Scottish winters was true. They were not for the faint of heart.

The biting, icy coldness wouldn't stop me from finding Benji. He was a hardy fellow with thick fur. Smart, too, so he'd find his way back to the castle if he didn't heed my call to return. But I didn't want him running in the wrong direction and getting confused. Frostbitten paws were no laughing matter, and darkness fell quickly this far up the country. Requesting a search party wouldn't be warmly greeted. And it most definitely didn't fit into the plan for a perfect wedding.

As I raced along, being careful where I put my feet to avoid a twisted ankle, the barking grew louder.

I hailed Benji again. "That's quite enough fresh air for you. I know the journey was a chore, but there will be roaring fires and treats inside."

I understood his desire to run and stretch his legs. We'd spent all day travelling up the country by train, and when we'd arrived at the station, we'd barely had time to inhale the frigid air before a large car whisked us into the depths of frozen Scotland.

Whose clever idea was it to have a winter wedding? If Juliet Augustine hadn't been such a solid friend during my Sunday school years, I'd have declined the invitation. The holidays were a hectic time for the pub trade, but she'd asked me to be her bridesmaid and had almost cried on the telephone when I'd not been enthusiastic about the request. And we hadn't seen each other in years, so I accepted, thinking we'd have fun reminiscing about the hours spent in a draughty church hall, stealing digestive biscuits, and not nodding off during Bible study.

After the wedding, I intended to enjoy plenty of long walks and hours curled in front of a roaring fire with a book. Not forgetting, I had the matter of our most unique pub to check on.

"Veronica! What's keeping you? We must get inside." My dearest friend and wedding guest, Ruby Smythe, was hunched inside the sleek black Bentley that had delivered us here. You could barely see her face since she was bundled up in thick layers to avoid the cold. And she wasn't alone.

I'd suggested such a long trip with an infant a foolhardy idea, but Ruby had insisted on bringing her new daughter, Grace. Grace could have remained behind with the army of helpers Lady M hired to ensure Ruby and Grace wanted for nothing, but Ruby had been determined to take the trip with her baby. Although she had consented to bringing one nanny, so she wouldn't miss all the fun.

"Benji is refusing to come back," I called out. "I'm not going inside until I've caught him."

"He'll sniff his way there," Ruby said. "He always knows how to find you. And it's not as if you can miss this place. I didn't realise how large the castle would be."

"They usually are. You go inside with Grace and make sure Juliet is behaving. Freddie, too. We don't need pre-wedding jitters causing havoc." I steadied myself as my foot slipped.

"I'm staying away from Juliet," Ruby said. "She was beastly to you when you had your last dress fitting. She said you'd gained weight, but she was the one unable to fasten her buttons!"

I waved to let her know I was listening, but I needed my full attention on finding Benji. When he got the scent of something fascinating, his stubbornness set in. I never held that against him, since it was a trait I also carried.

There was a rustle in a bush nearby. Got him! I dashed over and yelped as a lean white hare rocketed away, moving so fast it was a blur.

I rifled through my coat pockets and extracted a handful of dog biscuits. "Benji! Treats."

He barked again, making me tense. That wasn't his happy-go-lucky bark to say he was having a joyful time. Benji was scared of something.

"Bark again. Let me know where you are. Are you hurt?" I yelled in a most unladylike fashion. When it came to keeping Benji safe, I cared nothing about manners, just that my most beloved dog was well.

My breath came out in puffs as I dashed towards a thicket of trees. It was gloomy under the branches, and I could barely see where I was going. Colder, too. It was as if I'd stepped through a door into a different world. One with a most unfriendly atmosphere.

This environment was for the wildlife, not a domesticated dog and a hungry journalist, who wanted nothing more than a hot mug of coffee and a shortbread biscuit. Maybe a tot of local whisky, too, to keep the chill out.

I threw out treats, hoping Benji's nose would detect them and he'd come running. I called his name several times. Eventually, I heard a whimper and a small, sad bark.

My hands fisted. If anyone was hurting my dog, I'd make them severely sorry. I stamped along, no longer caring how unwelcoming this woodland was. I would find Benji.

Benji yipped again, and a second later, he was flying towards me, his tail down and his ears whipped back against his furry head.

A large shadow loomed behind him, causing me to tense in surprise. I couldn't see what caused that shadow, but it had four legs and was snorting.

I gestured to Benji, my heart pounding. "Hurry! Run!"

The second Benji was close enough so I could touch him, I turned, and we ran together. My boots held firm as my arms pumped. Benji kept up, leaping through the snow with the grace of a dog half his age.

We didn't stop running until we were almost back at the Bentley.

By this time, Ruby had stepped out of the vehicle, Grace swaddled under her thick winter coat, while the nanny hovered nearby, hunched over and not looking happy about all the snow. They stood with a giant of a man sporting a large, well-maintained, dark beard. His hands were knuckled against his hips as he roared with laughter at something Ruby said, his gaze affectionate on the sleeping infant. His green kilt left his sturdy knees exposed to the freezing weather, which didn't appear to bother him.

They turned to me, their faces morphing into surprise as they saw my panicked expression and the speed I moved with Benji.

"Good heavens! Is something wrong?" Ruby asked.

"I believe Benji startled an animal," I gasped. "It chased him."

The man scratched his beard. "Could it have been a deer? Or we have wild boars, but they wouldn't want to eat your wee dog. I suppose he could have scared it. They charge when angered. But I've not seen a boar around these parts for a while."

I looked over my shoulder. Whatever had chased us was gone, so I took a moment to compose myself and check on Benji. Now we were away from the immediate threat, he was calm and happy to take the treats I offered.

"Veronica, this is Angus Stewart," Ruby said.

I remembered my manners and shook Angus's hand. "Veronica Vale. It's a pleasure to meet you in person. We've spoken on the telephone many times." Angus was Augustine Castle's estate manager, having taken over the role a few years ago when the last chap retired after thirty years of loyal service.

"That we have," Angus said with a warm smile. "And likewise. All three of you. I didn't know we'd be hosting a young one."

"The child was a last-minute addition." I tried not to wrinkle my nose. Grace was a sweet little thing and mostly well-behaved, but I'd much rather have a puppy accompany us.

"It's no trouble fitting in such a wee bairn," Angus said. "And I've a fondness for children."

"Do you have many?" Ruby asked.

"I've not had the time to settle into family life. It'll come around." A wistful look entered his eyes. "Is this your first visit to Augustine Castle?" He gestured to the castle standing in front of us, its weathered stone walls dusted with freshly fallen snow. The turrets and conical towers were crowned with frost, and icicles clung to the ancient battlements.

"I've never been before," Ruby said.

"Juliet has spoken with great affection of her childhood stays here," I said. "I've been once, but many years ago. My father enjoyed his visits to Scotland. He always talked about the delicious whisky, and he enjoyed sampling the local offerings to sell at the Thistle Inn."

"I never had the pleasure of meeting him, but I heard from my predecessor that he was a fine man," Angus said. "I'm sorry for your loss."

"Thank you. He was the very best of men," I said. "And I feel remiss for not visiting sooner."

"We're a long way from London, so we don't take offence that you've not been for a visit," Angus said. "We're happy to have you here. And I hear you'll be staying on after the wedding. Having yourself a wee holiday."

"Yes! We need to get this headache out of the way before we can enjoy ourselves." Ruby gasped. "Oh, sorry. I shouldn't have said that out loud. The wedding will be delightful. I'm honoured Veronica chose me to be her guest."

"You don't have a gentleman friend accompanying you?" Angus asked me.

"My gentleman friend is stuck in Kent," I said.

Jacob Templeton had been my intended wedding guest, but bad weather in the southeast had prevented him from travelling up to London in time, so Ruby had gallantly stepped in. She was well-versed in the wedding plans, since she'd insisted on accompanying me to dress fittings with Juliet whenever an opportunity presented itself.

"That's a pity, but I'm sure you ladies will have a wonderful time," Angus replied.

"Once the wedding is over, I'm certain we will," I murmured, much to Angus's amusement. "But we must endure such events for old friends."

Angus's expression shifted to merriment. "If you ladies feel brave, you're welcome to sample a drop of our finest whisky from the local distillery. Although I know the Thistle Inn keeps an excellent collection of malts."

Ruby scrunched her nose. "I prefer a martini. My beastly doctor had me on rations, but now Grace is here, I'm a free woman."

"As free as one may be with a helpless infant to care for," I muttered.

Ruby huffed at me. "Oh, hush. Less of that. You said just last week how pretty you thought Grace was."

"My exact words were she looks less squashed but still has pudgy arms."

"Veronica! Don't be a horror, or you won't be her godmother."

I bit my tongue. Grace was acceptable but would be much more interesting when I could take her on long hikes and we could explore the wonders of the world together.

Angus chuckled. "Ladies, allow me to show you to your rooms. After such a long journey, you must want to relax."

"That's kind of you. Isn't Angus charming, Veronica?" Ruby fluttered her long lashes and tossed her hair, even though it was squashed under a hat. She was ever the incorrigible flirt, infant or not.

"He is the epitome of charm." I glanced over my shoulder again, but there was no sign of the creature that had pursued Benji, who sat alert but happy by my feet, so I knew we were in no danger.

"Don't worry about our unfriendly woodland resident. I'm sure whatever it was won't be back." Angus gestured for us to follow him to the grand wooden castle doors. "I've already dealt with your bags, so let's get you inside, and you can thaw out. You're the last to arrive today. The remaining guests will be here tomorrow morning."

I lingered by the door as Ruby hurried inside with the nanny beside her, chatting to Grace and admiring the entrance hall.

"Is something worrying you, lassie?" Angus asked when I didn't hurry after them into the welcoming warmth.

"I'm sure it wasn't a deer or a wild boar that chased us. It was too large. And there was an odd huffing snort. It was almost dog-like."

Angus's dark gaze sparkled. "Wherever there's an old building such as this fine castle, there's always a legend to go with it."

I arched an eyebrow. "What legend would that be?"

Angus chuckled again. "You had a close encounter with the Terror of Augustine Castle."

Chapter 2

Sitting in front of a blazing open fire in the opulent drawing room finally thawed out my toes. Benji was safely snuggled close to my feet, snoozing after treats and his mini adventure.

"Tell us more about this Terror of Augustine Castle." Ruby sat beside me on the luxurious plaid sofa. We had warm blankets over our knees, and mugs of hot chocolate had been delivered by a member of the immaculately turned-out household staff.

"It's an old and strange legend." Angus had ensured we were settled and then entertained us with a walk around the castle before leading us into the drawing room. Grace and the nanny were upstairs, getting everything unpacked and ensuring Grace had a nap.

"Don't keep us in suspense," Ruby said.

Angus prodded the logs in the expansive fireplace before settling the poker back into place. "The legend states that a fearsome beast appears close to the castle just before a tragedy occurs."

From his tone, I could tell he was teasing, but I was intrigued and about to ask more when hurried footsteps approached the room.

"That's quite enough of that, Angus. There will be no tragedies here!" Juliet Augustine strode into the room, an armful of silky fabric clutched against her chest and her curly blonde hair sporting a glittering tiara. "Everything will be utterly perfect. Veronica is here to make sure that happens."

I did my best to repress a grimace. As much as I adored my friend, Juliet had presented an exasperating level of demands with her wedding to Sir Frederick Galton the Third, an obscenely wealthy bachelor she'd been associating with for several years.

"I saw that!" Juliet placed the fabric on the back of a chair.

We embraced, and Ruby received a brief cheek kiss.

Juliet settled her hands on her hips, a look of disgruntled exasperation on her narrow face. "I'm so glad you're here. It appears I'm organising this entire wedding on my own."

"Where's Constance?" Ruby asked.

"I hope you haven't frightened off your hostess," I said.

"As if I would. She's doing something with the flowers," Juliet said with a dramatic sigh.

We were the same age, but her love of the latest fashions and makeup made her look younger than her thirty years. "I told her she has the wrong shade of white."

"There are different shades of white?" Angus asked.

"Over one hundred and fifty," Juliet said with a definitive, dainty sniff.

"And Juliet would know since she's looked at all of them," I said. "We had three weeks of exhausted florists presenting Juliet with the same flowers. All of them white!"

"They were not the same flowers. They were unique." Juliet peered at me. "Don't you dare ridicule my special day, or I'll set Freddie on you."

"Who do I need to have a word with, my dear?" Sir Frederick Galton the Third, Freddie, to his friends, strode into the room, his tailored grey three-piece suit failing to disguise his lanky form. He was a pale chap with wispy blond hair and a receding chin. Constance Bell, their chosen society hostess, accompanied him, carrying a bundle of papers and failing to hide her exhaustion, stumbling as she walked.

"Veronica is being mean. Tell her she's not to poke fun at us." Juliet sounded much younger than her years. I blamed that on her parents overindulging her with too much private education abroad. "This is my day, and she's not spoiling it. She's jealous because she has no husband."

"Darling, perhaps you shouldn't," Freddie murmured, with an apologetic glance my way. "And let's not mention a lack of husbands. After all, we all know of Mrs Smythe's tragedy."

"Oh, don't mind me." Ruby had the good grace to blush and look away. Grace had arrived after a lusty experience or ten with a rogue in the entertainment industry. To ensure Ruby's reputation wasn't sullied, we'd concocted a tale of a love lost during the Great War, mainly at the insistence of Ruby's forthright and influential employer, Lady M.

I pulled my shoulders back. "Perhaps marriage isn't for everyone."

"And I've had several proposals, but I'm waiting for the right chap to whisk me off my feet," Ruby said.

"Surely not so soon after you lost your dear husband." Juliet looked aghast. "Although with a child, I pity you. Few men will want such a burden."

Freddie drew in a sharp breath. "My dear, many men would—"

"Freddie, tell them my perfect wedding will not be tinged with envy green."

"It's *our* wedding, my love. And Veronica nor her friend will spoil it." Freddie kissed his fiancée's cheek, which appeared to do little to appease her heightened colour.

I gently squeezed Ruby's arm and leaned in close, keeping my voice low. "This will be over soon. Then we can relax and enjoy ourselves."

"I'll be jolly well relieved when this special day is over and done with," Ruby muttered. "The only thing I'm truly looking forward to is the food. And the dancing. And perhaps enjoying the men in their kilts. There's something about a kilt that makes one go weak at the knees. Perhaps I'll have a holiday fling. A Highland fling!"

I tapped her leg. "I think you've had enough flings for the time being, don't you? Or do you want another Grace to arrive?"

She pursed her lips. "Perhaps I'll just look. For now."

Juliet clapped her hands, making me jump. "Enough dawdling. I have fabrics for you to look at."

"Are those bridesmaids' dresses?" I asked with a degree of suspicion, sensing what was coming. "It's too late to change things. The wedding is in three days."

Ruby nodded. "The only thing we should focus on is enjoying your bridal rituals."

"These aren't the dresses!" Juliet tutted. "I must have wedding sashes. It's a Scottish tradition to wear the family colours. Veronica, stand up. I need to check the colours against your skin tone. I don't want you looking sallow."

The very nerve of the woman! Perhaps it was time to let this friendship fade into the background. It was a pity. We'd been close in Sunday school and remained in touch with regular letters and the occasional luncheon when time and location allowed.

A telephone rang in a distant part of the castle, and a moment later, footsteps approached, and a smartly turned-out butler entered the drawing room.

"I'm sorry to disturb you, but I've had word that the trains bringing in the wedding guests have stopped," he said.

"What's that?" Lord Robert Augustine, Juliet's uncle, ambled in. He was a tall chap of sixty with a wandering eye and even freer hands where the ladies were concerned. I'd avoided several grabs when we'd met at a dinner party Juliet had arranged so the wedding guests could form an acquaintance before the day arrived.

"There's been a train delay," Freddie told him. "Oh, what rotten luck."

"I heard more bad weather was rolling in," Angus said. "It must have caught up with your guests as they made their way up the country."

"What a terrible business." Lord Robert was inspecting Ruby's decolletage before nodding in approval and helping himself to a shortbread biscuit from a plate close to the fire.

"We'll send cars for them," Freddie said. "How many do we need?"

"A party of forty was travelling from Hampshire and another sixty from London," Juliet said, her face pale. "Where did the trains divert to?"

"Nottingham. There was a derailment further up the line," the butler said. "No trains are leaving until further notice."

"Nottingham! That's unacceptable. My friends and family must be here. My parents have already let me down by not attending due to the poor travel conditions. No one else can miss my wedding." Juliet threw up her hands and squeaked. "Surely, the weather can't want to jinx us, too!"

"What else is jinxing your wedding?" Ruby asked with a touch of tartness. "It appears you got everything you demanded."

I focused on the delicious shortbread and hid a smile. Juliet had a heart of gold, but her fretting in the lead-up to this wedding, which had been two years in the planning, would try a saint's patience.

"I don't make demands. I make reasonable requests!" Juliet scowled at Ruby. "Veronica refused to wear a tartan bridesmaid dress. Freddie's best man stepped down because he lost his voice. And I haven't forgiven Veronica for that dreadful haircut."

I touched the ends of my recently trimmed bob. "I like it. It tucks neatly behind my ears."

"I wanted nothing to change before my wedding," Juliet said. "A new hairstyle is change! You didn't ask my permission before going to the hairdresser."

My eyebrows lifted. "I needed permission to cut my own hair?"

Juliet flapped a hand in the air. "The style doesn't go with your tiara. You're wearing my family's heirlooms on your head, so you can't look ghastly. My photographs will be in the society pages of every newspaper."

My hands clenched, and I inhaled sharply. Old friend or not, I'd endured quite enough of this nonsense.

Ruby looked at me, her eyes wide. "Have another shortbread biscuit and take a deep breath."

"It's of no matter," Juliet said. "My hairdresser has styled princesses, so I'm certain she will fix that travesty."

Constance gently cleared her throat. She was a smartly turned-out hostess in her mid-thirties who must have the temperament of an angel, having to deal with Juliet and her rants. "I am sorry, but there's been a tiny problem with the harpist."

"Don't tell me, she lost her harp in transit and will have to play the wedding march on a borrowed mouth organ," Juliet snapped.

"She cancelled the booking because of the weather," Constance said in her usual soft-spoken lilt. "I'm looking into getting a replacement, but so late in the day..."

"How very dare she!" Juliet said. "Do you see now, Freddie? We're jinxed! What have we done so wrong to ensure our wedding turns into a Shakespearean tragedy?"

"Not everything has gone wrong." Ruby gestured for me to eat the shortbread before I said something I'd regret. "We have my bridal scavenger hunt in the grounds to look forward to."

"A scavenger hunt? Why would you arrange such a thing?" Juliet asked.

"We discussed it at length at the dress fitting." Ruby looked startled. "I suggested something fun, and you agreed I could plan an adventure. I even spoke to Constance about it on the telephone."

"Oh, I forgot." Juliet's scowl deepened. "I suppose it'll work up an appetite before our pre-wedding tasting dinner."

"I'd advise against going outside," Angus said. "With the weather closing in, I don't want anyone lost in a blizzard."

Juliet glowered at him and exhaled slowly. "You're saying I can't have my planned bridal rituals that I've been so looking forward to?"

Ruby gave an indignant snort, and I passed her a biscuit.

Freddie wrapped a comforting arm around Juliet's shoulders, which she shrugged off with disdain. "We have our delicious dinner to look forward to. That'll be splendid. Chin up. Our wedding will be the opposite of a Shakespeare tragedy."

"Chin up! The way things are going, someone will choke on a chicken bone and perish." Juliet turned and stomped out of the room.

Freddie looked at me with a helpless expression. "Gosh. Did I do something wrong?"

"You'd better go after her," I said. "You appear to be the only one Juliet can tolerate."

"Barely," Ruby muttered out of the corner of her mouth.

Angus overheard and failed not to laugh as Freddie dashed after Juliet, her ever-devoted beau.

I shook my head and sighed. Relationships were complicated. I was glad mine was such smooth sailing. Jacob had been a thorn in my side for a long time, but once we'd stopped locking horns, we'd discovered how wonderfully matched we were. I'd miss his company, but I'd promised him I'd telephone that evening and update him on our journey. And he was working on a fascinating case involving a stolen painting in his role at our private investigation agency in Kent, so I was intrigued to learn of his progress.

"I told you I want another room. Do you have cloth ears?" A cut-glass, angry voice drifted along the corridor. "And move my luggage immediately. That room is draughty. If I catch a cold, I'll have your job."

"Uh-oh! Sulky Sophia is on her way," Ruby said. "I don't know why Juliet asked her to be a bridesmaid, too. I thought you said they couldn't stand each other."

"Lady Sophia had Juliet as her bridesmaid," I said. "She felt obliged to return the favour. And they're cousins, so Juliet couldn't ignore her."

"She must be regretting that decision," Ruby said. "Lady Sophia's sour face will ruin the photographs. I didn't see her smile once at the dress fitting we attended."

"And she was full of spite at the dinner," I whispered. "It seems she's brought her venom with her."

Lady Sophia Merryweather stomped into the room, her dark eyes ablaze with fury and her nose turned up. Behind her was a surly faced man in his fifties, wearing a flat cap and damp boots that left prints on the floor.

"Will someone talk sense into this fool of a man?" Lady Sophia said, not addressing anyone in particular.

"Whatever is the problem?" Angus asked smoothly, hurrying over.

"He's refusing to move me," Lady Sophia said. "And from the way he is talking, you would think he, not the family, owns the castle. I should fire him for his disobedience."

"Don't mind old Gregor." Angus gave the exasperated-looking man a friendly pat on the shoulder. "He's been here for decades. This is his home."

"I'm certain his name is not on the deeds," Lady Sophia sniped. "And he should know his place. I always have the same room when I visit."

Gregor ducked his head. "I was just telling the lady it's not my job to let her change bedrooms. I'm the groundskeeper, so my place is outdoors."

"That's quite right. You prefer the great outdoors, don't you, my good man?" Angus said. "Lady Sophia, if the room is not to your liking, I'll find you another. You have twenty bedrooms to choose from. They are at your disposal."

Lady Sophia fluttered her eyelashes at Angus. "I knew I'd find a man with sense in his head. Come along then. Let's not dilly-dally." She barely acknowledged anyone else as she glided out of the room.

"I'd better make sure her ladyship has everything she desires," Angus said with a wink as he led a muttering Gregor out of the room.

"With so many people unable to get here, this will be a small wedding," Ruby said after they'd left.

"I prefer a smaller party," I said. "There is less noise and small talk to contend with."

"The handsome single chaps had better put in an appearance. I want a full dance card." Ruby glanced at Lord Robert and frowned. He'd nodded off in a chair close to the fire, biscuit crumbs on his white shirt.

"So long as you and Benji are beside me, and Juliet and Freddie finally get their happily ever after, that's all I care about," I said. "Friends, family, and good times."

"And no strange creatures chasing you out of the woods." Ruby shuddered. "We're here for a wedding, not a funeral."

I laughed. "The way Juliet is behaving, I'm uncertain everyone will survive this happy event."

Chapter 3

"Are you sure about this?" I checked the time on the softly ticking grandfather clock in the hallway. It was almost time for the pre-wedding dinner, and my stomach eagerly looked forward to a grand feast.

"I asked Angus. He said that provided we stay within the stone walls of the herb garden, we can have a scavenger hunt for thirty minutes," Ruby said. "Please join in. I spent hours preparing the clues, and it'll be no fun if you're not there."

"I'll do it if Juliet is happy to take part," I said. "After all, this is her special day."

Ruby wrinkled her nose. "As she keeps reminding us. We'll convince her to let down her hair and remember why we're here."

"She doesn't know we're going outside for her bridal rituals?" I paused from extracting my thick winter coat from the hallway cupboard.

"Juliet will be game. She's simply lost in the wedding arrangements," Ruby said.

"Something you won't catch me doing anytime soon."

"You will me! I'll find the perfect eligible bachelor, and we'll be blissfully happy together for the rest of our lives," Ruby said. "It'll be marvellous. He'll adore Grace and make the perfect husband and father."

I hid a small smile and good-naturedly shook my head. Ruby had disastrous luck in picking the right gentlemen. She went for the most handsome and the most caddish of the bunch.

But no matter what I said, Ruby never listened to me about choosing a sensible sort with a steady job and good morals. After all the fizz and fun imploded, I'd nurse her broken heart and have her swearing off men for at least five minutes until it all began again.

Perhaps now that Grace was here, Ruby would be a little more sedate, but her actions so far proved nothing had changed.

"You gather the bride and the rest of the party," I said. "I need to telephone Jacob before it gets any later."

Ruby's eyes sparkled. "He'll force you along the aisle one of these days." She dashed off before I could correct her, leaving me with Benji.

The castle's only telephone was located in the hallway, close to the main entrance, so once I'd gathered my coat, I settled in to make my call.

The telephone crackled to life after what felt like an eternity of waiting for the operator to connect us. "Jacob? Are you there?"

"Veronica? Can you hear me? This blasted line is dreadful," he said.

"Yes, I can just about make you out through all that static." I pressed the receiver closer to my ear. "How are you managing with the snow?"

"Oh, splendidly. Nothing like being trapped whilst my partner gallivants off to Scotland without me." His tone was dry, but I heard the warmth beneath it. "The trains are still cancelled, so there'll be no chance of me joining you in time. This weather shows no signs of letting up."

"I suspect you're rather enjoying yourself, focusing on the case, and not having to make such an arduous journey," I said.

"I'd much rather be with you." There was a pause filled with crackling. "Now then, tell me about the castle. Any mysterious happenings? Haunted suits of armour clanking about?"

I laughed despite myself. "Nothing quite so dramatic, though there is a most extraordinary collection of medieval weaponry you'd be fascinated by."

"And the wedding is still ticking along?"

"With a few shortcomings, including most of the guests failing to arrive." I sighed softly. "The grounds are glorious, though. We'd have had a wonderful time exploring."

"Perhaps Scotland can be our honeymoon destination."

I chuckled. Wedding talk was emerging more frequently with Jacob. I had to think of something to distract him. "What of your stolen painting case? Any progress with the theft?"

"Ah, now that's where things become interesting." His voice took on that particular quality it always did when he was onto something. "I had an enlightening conversation with the owner's assistant. It seems our man had specific knowledge about the security arrangements."

"An inside job, then?"

"Very much so. Though proving it is another matter entirely. I say, this line really is appalling. Are you still there?"

"Just about." The line crackled violently.

"Veronica? What was that?"

"We're fighting a losing battle with this wretched connection," I said, raising my voice. "Stay warm and don't do anything too adventurous without me."

"I shall endeavour to contain my wild impulses until your return." His voice faded in and out. "Give Benji a scratch behind the ears from me, will you?"

"Of course. He's already had quite an adventure," I said. "I'll tell you all about it when we return home."

"I look forward to it. Enjoy the wedding and safe travels back to…"

The line disconnected with a final, decisive crackle.

It hadn't been the perfect conversation, but I was glad Jacob was safe. The office had room for him to sleep in, so he'd be fine for a few days until the trains started up.

I peered out a window and frowned. I wasn't convinced these bridal games were sensible. Snow had steadily fallen for hours, and a brisk breeze had picked up, flinging snow up the castle walls in heaping drifts.

"Where are you off to?" Angus strolled along the vast hallway, still wearing his kilt and holding a whisky glass.

"Ruby is convinced we need a jolly good adventure." I peered at his knees. "Don't you get chilly?"

He chuckled. "I'm a born-and-bred Scotsman and proud of it. I suppose you don't see many kilts in London."

"It's uncommon."

"Kilts are practical." Angus bent his knees, grinning broadly. "There's room to move."

"This time of year, I'm always in thick stockings. That's what you call practical. I can walk in all weather."

"I'll have to get myself a pair if you think they'll suit me." Angus chuckled. "Have you had time to visit the inn?"

"I peeked in earlier, and everything looked to be in order." My late father had purchased the Thistle Inn many years ago. He'd excelled at finding and purchasing rundown pubs and inns and turning them into profitable ventures. This venture was unique, though, and was less about the money generated and more about the fact that he'd been charmed by the thought of having a pub inside a castle.

"There's little to see," Angus said. "As instructed, your landlord, Tommy, closed yesterday so as not to disturb the wedding. The locals aren't happy, but they'll survive a few evenings without their favourite tipple. And this isn't the time of year for tourists, so you don't need to worry about the till being empty."

I'd not been pleased to shut the inn. It would mean a loss of earnings, even if that were small, but Juliet had begged me, which had turned mildly threatening when she said she only wanted family and close friends at her wedding, not drunken strangers lurking about and making fools of themselves.

I'd conceded in the name of friendship and for a quiet life. After all, it was only a week of closure, so it wouldn't badly disrupt business. And with all this snow, only the hardiest of souls would brave the roads for a dram of whisky.

"I'll visit properly tomorrow," I said. "It's partly why we arrived early. I can inspect the business records to ensure all is well. And I'm meeting Tommy after the wedding. He has a few ideas for the place."

"Tommy is a fine landlord. Everyone likes him." Angus nodded. "Very good. So, what adventure do you have planned for now?"

"Ruby's scavenger hunt."

Angus looked startled. "Haven't you checked outside? The snow stacks up quickly when it's this cold."

"Oh! Well, naturally. But Ruby said you'd agreed to it."

His brow creased. "I don't recall that conversation. I've even sent the staff home so they're not trapped. Snow may be beautiful, but it's dangerous if you're unused to it."

"Are you saying Ruby didn't speak to you about our outdoor scavenger hunt?"

"I'd remember if that pretty face wanted my attention." He grinned broadly.

I sighed. "Ruby jolly well lied to me!"

"Aye, I reckon she did. But all for a good cause," Angus said. "It's bitter out there, though. If you're only used to London winters, the cold will suck the air out of your lungs and freeze your teeth."

I grimaced. "That sounds unpleasant. Ruby still wants to venture out, and she's determined when she sets her sights on something."

"The lassie will end up with frostbite on the end of that pretty nose." Angus shook his head. "How about I lend you a hand to persuade her to give up?"

I tilted my head, seeing the gleam of mischief in Angus's eyes. "What do you have in mind?"

Chapter 4

"There are deadbolts on all external doors. Inside and out," Angus said. "The family likes to be secure. I can sneak out and slide across the deadbolts. When Ruby tries the doors, she'll find them shut, and you can state that the cold must have frozen the locks and swollen the wood. Then she can only blame the weather for stopping you from having fun."

"It would stop any arguments," I said. "And I don't want frostbitten toes on the wedding day. Frozen blue toes would set the wrong tone."

Angus tapped the side of his nose. "Leave it to me."

Ten minutes later, Ruby was tugging on the hulking, ancient carved wooden main door. I stood beside her, along with Juliet, Lady Sophia, and Constance, who'd been encouraged to join us to make up the numbers. Benji was also there. Grace was wisely still asleep, having been tucked in by her nanny.

"Will somebody lend me a hand with this wretched thing?" Ruby gave a most unladylike grunt as she leaned back.

"The wood must be sticking because it's so wet," I said with an air of innocence I impressed myself with.

Ruby grunted again. "If we pull hard enough, we'll get the thing open. Come along, ladies. A tiny amount of snow won't defeat us. We have important bridal rituals to complete."

We each tried the door and then attempted a group effort. I felt the door give, but fortunately, the outside deadbolt held.

"Another jinx!" Juliet said with an unhappy huff. "And the dratted weather is getting worse by the second. I suppose I shouldn't mind. When I said I wanted a pre-wedding gathering, I meant a trousseau party, where we could sip tea, nibble on cake, and you could all admire my extensive plans."

"Don't you mean a spinster party?" Lady Sophia stifled a yawn.

"I despise that word. I may be thirty years of age, but I am most definitely not a spinster," Juliet said.

"We can't give up! This is one of your last nights as an unmarried lady," Ruby said. "Don't you want to enjoy yourself?"

"Of course I do. And I know how I plan on enjoying myself." Juliet leaned forward and beckoned us all closer. "I've been on the strictest of diets to ensure I fit into my wedding gown."

"I thought you looked drawn," Lady Sophia said. "You've taken the pale and innocent bride-to-be look too far. I feared you had consumption."

"I look like the perfect bride," Juliet said sharply. "But I'm finished with the restriction. All I want to do tonight is eat. And if I eat too much and split the seams of my gown, it'll be too late for Freddie to refuse to have me as his bride."

Ruby gave a startled laugh. "Good for you."

"Let's abandon this outdoor nonsense and prepare for this evening's merriment, shall we?" Juliet said. "I have a fabulous dress I simply must showcase."

After some grumbling from Ruby about all the time she'd wasted, everyone was glad to head upstairs to their bedrooms, remove their bulky outdoor clothing, and prepare for a sumptuous dinner.

"Are you attending the pre-wedding dinner?" I asked Constance as she walked behind us up the stairs.

She hesitated. "No. I still have a long list of things to check. Nothing can go wrong."

"You must make time to eat," I said.

"I insist you join us," Ruby said. "There's barely anyone here, and Juliet has been running you ragged."

"She has a point to prove." Lady Sophia was ahead of us but had stopped at the top of the stairs.

"About what?" I asked.

Lady Sophia's smile was cat-like. "Most people in high society say this marriage won't last more than a year."

"Hush! You don't want to make the bride angry." I glanced down the stairs, grateful not to see Juliet.

"It's true." Lady Sophia gave an elegant shrug. "Juliet is taking her nervousness out on Constance."

"Which is unfair," Ruby said. "The least we can offer her is delicious food."

"Don't worry about me. I'm used to particular brides," Constance said with an air of good-naturedness that Juliet didn't deserve.

"I'd still like you to join us," I replied. "You'd be helping us. With so many people still stuck en route to the wedding, we'll look foolish scattered around such a vast dining table."

"Why don't we invite that rude groundsman to join us as well?" Lady Sophia turned and drifted away. "Make the entire event shambolic."

"I'll be there if I can, but please don't wait for me," Constance said after a second of hesitation. "I need to find a quiet space to work without being disturbed."

"By Juliet?" Ruby raised a knowing eyebrow.

Constance had the grace to duck her head rather than affirm Ruby's suspicions.

"You're welcome to use the private office at the Thistle Inn," I said. "It's closed until after the wedding, and Juliet won't think of looking for you in there."

Constance's tired eyes lit up. "That would be marvellous. If it doesn't put you to any trouble, I'll be in your debt."

"There's no need for that," I said. "Ask Angus for the key. He has keys to all the rooms in the castle."

After Constance thanked me again, she hurried off to locate Angus.

We retired to our respective bedrooms, and although it only took me ten minutes to change and tidy my hair, I had to endure fifteen minutes of Ruby fussing around me with her extensive makeup collection before she declared I was fit for company.

After checking on Grace, who was fast asleep, her nanny watching over her, we descended the stairs.

I wore a fine beaded dress in deep blue that Ruby had chosen for me. She was much more proficient at selecting suitable evening wear, given I had a mind for stomping around muddy fields in boots and tweed with not a care in the world.

Ruby wore a stunning beaded gown of pale green, cut smartly to hide the recent change in her figure.

Even Benji looked dapper with a plaid neckerchief I'd purchased especially for the wedding.

We paused at the dining hall entrance to take in the grandeur. The high ceilings arched above us, and the polished wooden floor gleamed. Massive chandeliers hung overhead, and a warm glow came from flickering flames in the enormous hearth.

A long dining table was set in the centre of the room, its white linen cloth spread with fine china, silver cutlery, and delicate glassware, ready for us to enjoy an evening of overindulgence and merriment.

"Do you think Angus will join us for dinner?" Ruby asked.

"I imagine not. He's the castle manager, not a family member or friend," I said. "It would be improper for him to attend."

"He has a relaxed way about him. Juliet and Lady Sophia appear at ease in his company."

"Whatever are you suggesting?"

"Nothing scandalous! But I was hoping to see him in that fabulous kilt again," Ruby said. "He looks smashing. Some men have ghastly, knobbly knees, but his knees are delicious."

I chuckled. Ruby always enjoyed over-romanticising a situation. "He seems rather taken with you, too. He was admiring your nose."

"My nose? Gosh. How exciting." Ruby jigged on the spot. "Despite being a fallen woman, I can still catch a handsome chap's eye."

"Hush, now. In this company, you aren't fallen, simply a tragic widow."

Ruby grimaced. "I don't like that description one bit."

"It's the story you concocted with Lady M, so we must stick to it."

She sighed. "Very well. But a tragic lady is still allowed a small flirtation, isn't she?"

"I'll allow a tiny one, but be delicate about it."

A second later, the rest of the party joined us. Juliet looked striking in a red silk dress with a white fur wrap draped around her narrow shoulders. Freddie had bravely donned a kilt, which he appeared uncomfortable in, and kept tugging at the hem as if he found his exposed flesh deplorable.

Lord Robert also wore a kilt, looking bemused, as if uncertain what he was doing in the castle. His gaze drifted to Ruby's chest, and he murmured something most unsuitable for polite company.

Lady Sophia appeared next, and I was glad to see Constance following her. It was only right that we included her. She'd worked jolly hard to ensure Juliet and Freddie's wedding ran smoothly, despite the bride's incessant demands. However, I wondered if Constance would have preferred her bed since she kept yawning.

Once we were settled around the table and our glasses full thanks to Freddie's attentiveness, Angus appeared. He served the first course of quail eggs and a lightly dressed olive salad. "My apologies, but I'll be your exclusive server this evening. I sent the staff home because of the bad weather."

Everyone agreed that was sensible, and despite Freddie insisting Angus join us, ably supported by Ruby, he declined, saying he needed to watch over things in the kitchen.

We tucked into our food, murmuring our approval while making small talk about the castle and the quality of the meal.

"I hope you're taking notes while you eat," Juliet said. "This menu will be served on my wedding day. If anything's not perfect, let me know. We still have time to make changes."

Constance's flinch and her haggard appearance didn't escape my notice. The poor woman. I hope she had a long holiday planned after this arduous job was over. Managing high society events must be pernickety.

Angus arrived and cleared the plates, his movements brisk but careful, the silver cutlery chiming softly as he stacked it.

Juliet rose as he left the room, smoothing her gown. "I'll just see that everything's in order. One can't be too careful with sauces and souffles. Our kitchen is excellent, but with everyone sent away, things could descend into chaos."

Ruby leaned towards me as Juliet disappeared after Angus. "She's ensuring he doesn't burn the food."

I hid a smile behind my napkin. "That will be interesting. Juliet knows less about managing a kitchen than I do."

While we waited for the next course, Lady Sophia dabbed delicately at her lips with her napkin and pushed back her chair. "I shall powder my nose and fetch another wrap. There's a draught at this table that could wake the dead."

Constance gave a faint nod and rose too. "I think I'll stretch my legs." She stifled another yawn and blinked rapidly, as if the effort of standing required concentration. "Goodness, I'm frightfully tired this evening."

"Perhaps the Highland air has caught up with you," I said.

"Or the wine," Ruby murmured, nodding at Constance's empty glass.

Constance gave a weak smile as she drifted out after Lady Sophia, her steps languid.

For a moment, the room fell quiet but for the crackle of the fire.

Lord Robert broke it with a genial cough. "Splendid course, that. Quite puts me in mind of the old housekeeper's efforts when I was a boy."

Freddie gave a polite chuckle. "I'm glad it met with your approval. We've spared no effort tonight. Only the best for your favourite niece."

"Indeed, indeed." Lord Robert reached inside his waistcoat and produced a slim silver pill case. He flipped it open, shook a small tablet into his palm, and popped it into his mouth. Lifting his glass, he washed it down with a generous gulp of claret.

Ruby tilted her head. "A remedy for the rich food?"

"Nothing of the sort. I have the constitution of a highland bull," he said easily, tucking the case away. "It's just a little assistance for a man who cannot fight the ravages of age forever. My physician swears by them."

Freddie raised an eyebrow. "You and your endless tonics. Which doctor sold you those?"

Lord Robert huffed out a breath. "An expensive one. But at my age, one takes help where one can find it."

"This is a subdued affair, don't you think?" Ruby whispered to me. "The wedding will be the same if the guests don't make it in time. I hope they get the trains running. There's still time for everyone to make it."

"We can't influence the weather," I replied. "It was always a risk, having a winter wedding, especially in Scotland. It's a stunning part of the country, but London would have been a more sensible choice."

"If my family had a castle instead of a crumbling country pile, I'd get married in it and show it off to everyone."

"I'd be happy with a local registry office," I murmured, "so long as they let Benji in."

"You're dreadfully unromantic," Ruby said with a tut.

"Perhaps that's why I remain happily unmarried."

"You're a catch, as the fine Mr Templeton has discovered. Lesser men fled when they got a taste of your sharp tongue."

"It's not sharp!"

Ruby gently snorted a laugh. "I've been sliced by it a time or two."

"Only when you do something impetuous."

"I'm never impetuous. Perhaps a touch impulsive, but what is life without fun?" Ruby placed her napkin on the table. "I must look in on Grace, and I need to change my stockings. These aren't sitting comfortably. And then I'm finding Angus and insisting he join us for the next course. We have the room, and we're not short of food."

"Check with Juliet before issuing such an invitation," I murmured. "She may not appreciate her castle manager joining the gathering."

"Provided Freddie keeps her entertained with his knobbly knee display, she'll barely notice. Besides, Juliet's not here to ask, so that option is unavailable to me. What a pity. I'll be back in a moment." Ruby dashed out of the room.

Ten minutes later, I was still at the table, accompanied by Lord Robert's gentle snores and Freddie's steady monologue about the disadvantages of Scottish architecture over solid London dwellings.

"Remarkable, isn't it?" he was saying, tugging his dinner jacket closer. "One could light every grate in the place and it would still feel like the inside of an icebox. I'm half convinced these old castles were designed to keep people chilled on purpose. Some ancient cure for over-heating tempers, no doubt."

I gave a sympathetic smile. "The draughts are part of the charm."

"Charm?" He gave a short laugh. "You, my dear Veronica, are far too charitable. If Juliet insists we live in a place like this after we're married, I shall invest in an overcoat company. There's money to be made in keeping one's bones warm. This castle requires a complete upgrade to its heating system. Engineers can do remarkable things these days."

Benji stirred under the table and shifted his head over my shoes, a welcome foot-warmer far superior to any thick sock. I bent to scratch his ears. "Benji agrees with me about the castle's charm. He's perfectly comfortable."

Before Freddie could reply, hurried footsteps echoed down the long corridor, the sound growing louder by the second.

The door burst open and Angus stumbled in, breathless, his face drained of colour.

"Good heavens, man." Lord Robert roused himself with a start, blinking owlishly. "What's the commotion? Did you burn the pheasant?"

Angus braced a hand against the doorframe. "You'd better come quickly. There's been a murder!"

Chapter 5

Freddie broke the stunned silence by knocking over his glass of wine.

I got to my feet, Benji instantly by my side. Lord Robert remained in his seat, staring open-mouthed at Angus.

Freddie stood and rushed over to Angus. "What happened? Who's dead?"

"I ... I don't know what happened."

Freddie shook him by the shoulder. "Gather your senses, my good fellow. Who do you think has been murdered?"

Angus shook himself. "Constance! I saw her body."

"Where is she?" I asked. "Unless you're absolutely sure Constance is dead, we may be able to assist her. I have basic medical training. So does Ruby."

"Constance is beyond saving," Angus said with a visible shudder. "She... she has a dagger sticking in her back."

I inhaled sharply. "Let's still check. I've stumbled across soldiers I was certain were gone, but they survived the most grievous battlefield injuries."

Angus looked away as he ran a hand down his face. "I can show you if you have the stomach for it, but you can't get near her."

"You're making no sense," Freddie said. "Where is Constance?"

"In the office in the Thistle Inn," Angus said. "And the door is locked from the inside."

"Then how do you know what happened to her?" I asked.

"I looked in through an outside window," Angus said. "Follow me, and I'll show you."

"Veronica should remain behind." Freddie glanced at me, his expression pinched. "This won't be pleasant for a lady."

"This lady is more than capable of inspecting a body," I said with more sharpness than I'd intended.

Freddie appeared suitably chastised and muttered an apology.

"This way," Angus said.

With a shocked silence lingering, we all followed Angus out of the dining room. He led us to the end of the corridor, under a carved archway, and into the silent body of the Thistle Inn. It was a small, dark space with low ceilings and scarred beams. The inn was almost as old as the castle and just as quirky.

"Constance asked you for the office key?" I said to Angus.

He nodded. "Earlier this evening, before dinner. She said you offered her the space to work."

"I did. I didn't think she'd make use of it this evening, though."

We stopped outside a pair of double oak doors that led into the office that sat at the back of the inn.

"She's on the other side." Angus's voice was hoarse.

Freddie tried both handles. "Where is the key?"

"Constance must have it on her," Angus said. "I tried to gain entrance, but those doors won't budge."

"Why would the girl lock herself in?" Lord Robert trailed over and peered at the doors.

"To avoid Juliet's demands," I murmured, more to myself than anybody else.

"We must get inside," Freddie said, a gleam of sweat on his upper lip. "As Veronica stated, it may not be too late to assist."

"Put your coats on and come outside," Angus said. "You'll see there's nothing we can do for the poor lass."

As we bundled ourselves into warm clothing, Ruby appeared and hurried to join us. "Whatever is going on? I returned to the dining room, and you were gone. I thought it was some sort of game."

"Something terrible has happened to Constance," I said, handing her a coat.

"Has she resigned? Walked out into the snow in a huff? I can't say I blame her after everything she's been through." Ruby glanced at Freddie and blushed.

"It's more serious than that," I said. "Angus believes Constance is dead."

Ruby gasped, and one hand fluttered against her chest. "Good grief. What are we doing standing around? And why are we going outside? Is Constance in the snow?"

Angus led us out as I updated Ruby. He gathered us around a window, through which a pale glow filtered from an inside light.

We peered in.

Constance lay face down on a desk, her unseeing eyes turned towards us and her hands splayed flat on either side of her head. An ornate dagger's hilt protruded from her back, and blood soaked her clothing.

"I don't feel quite right." Freddie staggered away from the window, a hand pressed against his stomach.

"Do these windows only open from the inside?" I asked Angus after taking a few deep breaths. Seeing a body always sent a shockwave of unpleasantness through oneself.

"You could pry one open from this side with the right tools, but not without badly damaging the wood."

I remained focused on the crime scene, not letting my shock get the better of me. "We must get inside the office."

"With your permission, I can break the door down. There's only one key, so that's how we get in. I can get Gregor to help," Angus said. "He's gone back to the stables."

I nodded. "Get on with it."

Angus marched away, the darkness quickly swallowing him.

I carefully tested the windows to see if they were loose in their frames, but they held fast. "If Constance had confronted someone attacking her, she'd have been standing. Her killer would have hit her from the front, not from behind."

"Which means she was caught off guard." Ruby's face was pale, but a determined glint shone in her eyes. She'd seen wartime horrors, too, and despite her flippant nature, she knew when to take life seriously.

"Dreadful, dreadful," Lord Robert kept muttering from his position in the open doorway leading back into the castle's warmth, but offering no useful commentary or suggestions of how to reach Constance.

Freddie staggered back to join us, wiping one hand across his mouth. "Let's get in the warm before we catch our death."

After taking a last look around, I agreed. Any evidence a person had lurked outside, watching Constance, was gone thanks to the strong winds and the heavy snow pelting down on us.

We bustled inside, stamping our feet and rubbing our hands together as we returned to the Thistle Inn. A few seconds later, Angus appeared with Gregor. They held sturdy axes.

Gregor nodded as he walked past us and waited for Angus's instructions before they set to work on the door, the sound of metal on ancient wood splintering the air.

Lady Sophia appeared in the doorway a few seconds later, alarm on her face. "Whatever's going on? Stop destroying our home!"

"I gave them permission. And we've no choice." I swiftly updated Lady Sophia about the grim discovery awaiting us behind the locked door.

She reeled back. "This must be a mistake."

"We've all looked through the window from outside," I said. "Angus is correct in what he saw."

Lady Sophia's brow furrowed. "If Constance was locked in the office alone, how did someone murder her?"

"The killer could still be in there!" Ruby looked around the inn. "We should arm ourselves."

"If he's hiding in there, we'll give him what for," Freddie said, having regained some colour since we returned inside. "This is jolly unfair. Constance was a capable lady and well-regarded as an elite event organiser. She never complained about a single thing."

"Not to her paying customers, she didn't," Ruby muttered to me.

"I was so focused on Constance that I didn't look around the rest of the office," I said. "It's not a large space, but there are places to hide. We may have a stroke of luck and catch our killer."

"We should find weapons," Ruby said.

"Whoever is hiding in there will be no match for us," Freddie said. "I boxed at university."

"Do you have guns on the premises?" Ruby asked.

"Good grief! We can't have an untrained female firing off rounds willy-nilly," Lord Robert spluttered.

"We have guns." Angus paused in his task. "They're locked up, though."

"Whatever is all this dreadful noise?" Juliet appeared in the entrance to the Thistle Inn. "Why are you all in here? Stop this instant. We need to return to my pre-wedding banquet."

Freddie dashed over and updated his bride-to-be on the tragic events. Juliet visibly sagged against him, her eyes wide with shock.

By this time, Gregor and Angus had made a sizable hole in the door.

"Move back. I'll look through," I said.

"Let me," Angus said.

"Your head is too large. That hole is big enough for me."

Angus reached through the hole and felt around. He sighed. "Constance didn't leave the key in the door. We'll have to keep going until the hole's big enough to clamber through."

"Before you do, let me peek," I persisted.

"What if someone is in the office?" Ruby gripped my arm. "They could try to take your head off."

Benji placed a paw on my leg, his usual whip-smart, fearless self. If anyone lurked behind that door waiting to attack, he'd bring them down. Especially if he thought the threat was directed towards me or Ruby.

I cleared the splinters with a bar cloth to ensure he wasn't hurt. "Benji! Through the hole." I gestured at the opening.

He sprang through with perfect precision, and I crouched to watch his reaction. Any hackles lifting or ears pricking and I'd know there was trouble waiting for us.

He took a moment to look around then headed to the desk at the back of the office, close to the open fireplace. His nose was up as he sniffed, aware of the scent of blood. After he'd inspected the room, he returned to the door and poked his head through for a congratulatory scratch, which he thoroughly deserved. He was a brave and reliable dog.

"Good boy!" I glanced up at Angus. "There's no one nefarious in there. Benji would have warned me of any danger. I'll squeeze through and attend to Constance. While I do, someone must telephone the police."

"You make the telephone call, Gregor," Angus said. "I'll continue here and widen the hole so we can all get in."

Gregor put down his axe and scurried away while Angus attacked the door again.

A few minutes later, I cleared more splinters before lifting one leg.

"Wait!" Ruby dashed over and slid a suit jacket around me, borrowed from Freddie. "You'll ruin your dress."

"That's the last thing I'm worried about," I said.

"You should be. It cost a small fortune," Ruby said.

I tucked the jacket around me and squeezed through the hole, landing on my hands first and then pulling through my legs.

Benji wagged his tail as I joined him in the office, although he was subdued, recognising that the scent of blood meant bad news.

I hurried to the desk and looked at Constance. She wasn't breathing. I checked for a pulse, but there was nothing. Her body was warm, so this had only just happened. She'd been away from the dining table for less than twenty minutes. How had someone committed this crime so swiftly? And why?

I glanced at the door, and a shiver of alarm plucked at my spine. Someone in this party must know what happened. Someone in the Thistle Inn was a murderer.

"Any luck?" Ruby called from the other side of the door. She crouched to look through the hole.

"Constance is dead," I said. "Whoever attacked her meant business. I don't think anyone would have survived this injury, no matter how swiftly help arrived."

There were several seconds of muttering, and hurried footsteps grew near, followed by muted male voices.

"Damn it!" Angus exclaimed. "We need them here."

I dashed over and peered through the hole. "What's going on?"

"There's no help on its way," Angus said grimly.

Chapter 6

"We must have the police here!" Juliet was almost hysterical, her voice high-pitched and squeaky. "There's a dead body in my inn!"

I decided now wasn't the time to mention that I owned the Thistle Inn, and Juliet's parents looked after this estate until she inherited it.

Gregor clutched his hat and shuffled his feet. "I'm sorry. The police have been called out as part of a search party for a missing group. Bleedin' visitors took it upon themselves to hike without making proper provisions. There's a worry they're freezing to death and need bringing home."

"The police won't have left the local station unattended," Freddie said with an undeserved air of confidence. "Who did you speak to?"

Gregor shuffled some more. "A young fellow. A volunteer, I think he said, although the connection was bad. Not a policeman. He didn't believe me when I spoke of a death, or maybe he couldn't hear. Either way, he asked me if I'd been drinking."

Lady Sophia tutted. "We shouldn't have sent the help to use the telephone."

Gregor flinched away. "He also told me the roads are impossible to travel on out this far, so he couldn't send anyone, even if there was a spare officer."

"This is outrageous! There must be someone in charge who can sort this dreadful business," Freddie said. "They wouldn't expect us to manage this situation on our own."

"If we were in London, things would be different," Lady Sophia said. "Whose delightful idea was it to have their wedding in the middle of nowhere?"

"Let's do what we can until the police arrive," I said, noticing the mottling rising up Juliet's neck as she glowered at Lady Sophia. "I'm sure the chap you spoke to took you seriously. Angus and Gregor, get the door open so we can inspect the office. And Angus, you know this room better than any of us, so you're in charge of noticing if anything is out of place."

He nodded. "I inspect it weekly, but Tommy will know the layout better than I do."

"But he's not here," I said. "And we can't summon him, since he's down in Somerset with family."

"What... what should we do with Constance's body?" Juliet whispered.

"We can't move her," I replied. "We don't want to contaminate any evidence that may assist the police with their enquiries."

"Evidence! What do we know about that?" Freddie asked.

"The murder weapon, for one," I said. "The police can do wonders with fingerprint analysis, so if our killer was clumsy or acted on impulse, they could have left a print behind. And items could be missing that may shine a light on why Constance is dead. Angus needs to check that."

"How do you know about fingerprints?" Lady Sophia lifted her chin, an interested glint in her eyes.

"Veronica is the one I told you about," Juliet said in a stage whisper.

"You gossip about so many of your friends, how am I supposed to pick one from the other?"

"Veronica is the one who writes for a newspaper," Juliet persisted, casting a guilty look my way. "I know you remember me telling you about her after the dress fitting."

"Ah! The one with an unhealthy interest in the dead." Lady Sophia peered down her nose at me. "The single one."

"She is very much not single!" Ruby sprang to my defence.

"I see no ring." Lady Sophia's gaze flickered over me. "And there was no talk of a chap at the dress fitting or party we attended."

"Perhaps tawdry baubles and small talk are of little consequence to me." I made a point of staring at the many diamonds adorning Lady Sophia's fingers. She fairly sparkled like a Christmas tree.

"It must take a curious chap to have an interest in someone who prefers the company of the dead to the living." Lady Sophia glanced at Juliet. "Wasn't that how you described her?"

Juliet flushed scarlet and lowered her head. "Those weren't my exact words."

"I have an inquisitive nature and a sharp mind, if that's what you're referring to," I said. "And my interest in the dead comes from my profession at the London Times. I write obituaries."

Freddie snapped his fingers. "Indeed, you do! And I enjoy them. Well, as much as you can enjoy reading about the dead. But you bring them to life if you see what I mean."

"I'll take that as a compliment," I said. "Now, let's focus on the recently deceased, shall we?"

"I'll get to work on the door," Angus said. "Gregor. You're with me."

Gregor picked up his axe again, and the men resumed their door-breaking efforts. The persistent pounding gave me a headache, but I used the time to explore the rest of the office before everyone else entered and disturbed the scene.

It was a grand space, if compact, with several ceiling-to-floor tapestries adorning the walls, clearly original, ancient, and most likely grossly expensive to make or purchase. The desk Constance was sprawled across dominated the room, alongside a grand open fireplace, with a large log stacked ready for burning, although it hadn't been lit.

With an ear-splitting crack, the door gave way. Angus and Gregor knocked through the final panels, ensuring everyone could gain access.

"I don't want to go in," Juliet said, her face sour milk pale. "It's too grisly."

"Stay out here with me, my love," Freddie said. "I'll protect you."

Juliet clung to his arm. "Protection! Do you think whoever did this to Constance is still prowling around?"

"If they are, I'm following the men with the axes." Ruby stepped over the broken wood and headed towards me. She leaned in close. "Did you find anything useful?"

I maintained my focus on the contents of the room. "Not as yet, but I only looked in briefly earlier today and wasn't committing anything to memory."

Angus and Gregor stood silently next to Constance's body, their heads bowed.

While that task occupied them, I led Ruby to the windows. "What do you see?"

She peered at the window, tilting her head like an eager cocker spaniel. "Nothing."

"Exactly. The wood is intact, with no sign of damage done on the inside of the frame," I said. "There were also no marks outside, so the killer didn't use this route to escape."

Ruby turned to the door. "Then how did they get in and out?"

"Here's the key." Gregor had moved back to the door and sifted through the splintered wood with his sturdily booted foot. He held up a metal key.

"Constance must have locked herself in," Angus said. "We knocked the key loose when we hit the door."

"It's strange she left dinner partway through to come here," Ruby said.

"Constance appeared tired," I remarked. "Perhaps she needed a quiet place to compose herself."

Angus sidled over. "I understand her position. I'm happy to see Miss Augustine and Sir Frederick married, but we've had no respite since the wedding announcement. Gregor has even taken to hiding in the woodshed or the old stables some days."

"The poor fellow," I sympathised.

Lady Sophia lingered outside the office door with Juliet, Freddie, and Lord Robert, all of them peering through the doorway with evident curiosity but with no desire to get any closer to a corpse.

"Are you sure there's no one else in there with you?" Lady Sophia asked. "Have you checked under the desk?"

"Benji would have sniffed out an intruder," I said. "He's an excellent scent hound."

"Perhaps the blood distracted him." Lady Sophia wrinkled her nose. "Even from here, it's most pungent."

"Come away from the door!" Juliet said. "It's making me light-headed just thinking about what happened."

Lord Robert and Freddie ignored her and, overcome with a bout of courage, edged into the room, though neither seemed eager to approach Constance's body and looked at everything else.

"What should we do while we wait for the police?" Freddie asked. "We still have dinner waiting for us. Although the next course will be cold."

"I can't eat after this!" Juliet exclaimed. "I wanted everyone to sample the wedding menu so Constance could make all my last-minute changes. What a bother. That won't happen now."

"If the dagger was lodged in Constance's belly rather than in her back, I'd suggest she fell on it to escape this wedding nightmare," Ruby whispered to me.

"Indeed. Let's go to the games room," I suggested, fearing Juliet was about to toss every shred of dignity into the snowstorm and have it whisked away if she grew more frantic and thoughtless with her comments. "It's comfortable, the fire is blazing, and we've all had a shock."

"There's also a well-stocked drinks cabinet," Angus said. "After this surprise, we need a stiff drink to settle the nerves."

Everyone agreed that was an excellent idea, and within minutes, we were settled in the games room, the door firmly closed. We were on edge, our nerves jangling at the possibility that a killer was on the loose.

I, however, was more concerned that the killer was in this very room.

"You should ask some questions," Ruby said quietly, leaning close on the sofa we'd settled on, Benji by my heel. "You're jolly good at getting people to open up when interviewing them for your obituaries."

"Perhaps we should leave this to the police."

"You have the skills to solve this." Ruby gently jabbed a finger into my ribs. "And I can tell you're itching to figure this out."

"I am curious. More to ensure our safety than anything else."

"You never allow an injustice to slide. Now is not the time to be opaque about your skills."

"Juliet will never forgive me if I spoil her wedding by turning this into a murder investigation," I whispered.

"Guest delays, a fearsome snowstorm, and a murder have already ruined the wedding. There's little more you can do to add to the tragedy."

I accepted the whisky Angus handed me, my gaze settling on each occupant for a few seconds. It was a small group, so finding the killer shouldn't be difficult. I was innocent of this crime. Ruby, too. Freddie and Lord Robert had been with me in the dining room, which ruled them out.

That left Lady Sophia, Gregor, Juliet, and Angus as potential killers.

I sipped my whisky, the warm liquid burning down the back of my throat. Smoothing my hands over my remarkably undamaged dress, I stood.

As I did so, Gregor lurched to his feet. "Lord above! I forgot the tunnels."

All eyes turned to Gregor, and his cheeks burned bright under so much scrutiny.

"Whatever are you talking about?" Lady Sophia asked. "Should you even be in here?"

"Of course he should," I said. "Go on, Gregor."

His gaze shifted to me, and he gulped. "The castle has old tunnels, so the servants could move around unnoticed by the household. There's a warren of them running alongside the main corridors."

"Oh! Excellent. Yes, good man." Angus slapped Gregor on the back. "I'd forgotten about the tunnels, too. Is there one connected to the Thistle Inn office?"

Gregor nodded. "The tunnel network services all downstairs rooms."

"Then what are we waiting for?" Ruby was already heading to the door. "Let's grab candles and torches and explore! That's where our killer is hiding."

Chapter 7

We were back in the office where Constance lay, standing in front of an ancient wooden door with a black, wrought-iron handle. I'd missed it when I'd first entered the office because a vast tapestry covered it.

"How far does this passageway go?" I asked Gregor.

"It follows the line of the main hallway, passing through two parlours, a dining room, and into the main kitchen," Gregor said.

"No one has used this route in years." I peered into a cobwebbed corner, the dust thick and undisturbed.

Angus nodded. "Anyone coming through this door would have given themselves away."

"Don't touch the handle," I said as he reached for it. "There could be fingerprint evidence."

Angus withdrew his hand. "We need to check the tunnels to be sure nothing's been missed."

"Use cloths or gloves to ensure we preserve evidence as best we can," I said.

"Someone must have slipped into the castle unnoticed and hid in this ghastly passageway, waiting to strike." Juliet shivered and rubbed her arms. "It's a madman, and he happened upon Constance first. We're all in danger!"

"How did this mysterious person access the castle?" I asked. "The roads are impassable. We only just made it in time before the snow set in, and no one would risk the journey on foot. They'd perish in the cold."

"They would have attempted it if they had no sense in their head," Juliet said. "Perhaps their urgent need to kill keeps them warm."

"Don't be ridiculous," Lady Sophia said.

"Could the killer have arrived earlier in the day?" Freddie asked. "He snuck in and waited for an opportunity to murder Constance."

"Why would anyone want her dead?" Ruby asked.

"It must have been bad luck," Angus said. "I reckon some blighter broke in, hoping to strike it lucky and steal the expensive wedding gifts that have been arriving all week. Constance disturbed him. Perhaps he made a noise in the tunnel or opened the door without realising anyone was in here. When he discovered the office occupied, he had no choice but to silence her."

Juliet trembled. "He could be hidden behind that door this very second, all wild-eyed and evil because he knows we're about to discover him."

"He'd be foolish if he were," I said. "We're hardly being stealthy, so he'd know the game is up."

"If I were the killer, I'd have tucked myself out of sight and waited for a chance to escape," Ruby said.

I turned to Gregor. "Do these tunnels run the entire length of the castle?"

He nodded. "Lower floors only, but you can get from the front to the back if you know which doors to access.

They're not used anymore since we have a smaller staff, and the family is agreeable to the servants being seen."

"If this was the killer's way in, and I'm not sure it was, whoever killed Constance must have intimate knowledge of this castle," I said. "Even Gregor forgot they were here."

"Not necessarily," Angus said after a brief pause. "It's common to have servant passages in larger castles. If they had knowledge of working in a castle or simply an interest in historical architecture, that would have given them a clue as to the layout of Augustine Castle."

"It must be a stranger," Freddie said. "It's the only logical conclusion. None of us wanted poor Constance dead!"

"Of course it was a stranger," Juliet agreed.

I arched an eyebrow and looked around the group. "What if there were a more logical conclusion?"

A silence twisted around the room, no one willing to state the possibility that a killer lurked in this very wedding party.

Freddie shook his head. "Come now, Veronica. I refuse to consider that anyone here did this. We know each other! We're friends or family."

"We don't know him." Lady Sophia pointed a pale finger at Gregor.

Gregor took a step back. "I'm ... I'm not involved."

"Gregor revealed the concealed door to us," I said. "Why would he do that if he used it to murder Constance?"

"Quite right. Gregor is part of this castle. This is his home. No more accusing anyone at this stage," Angus said. "I suggest we split into pairs and search the tunnels.

None of us will rest until we know there isn't some madman on the loose."

"I agree," Freddie said.

"I'm coming with you," Juliet said.

"Would you like to accompany me, my dear?" Lord Robert asked Lady Sophia.

She grimaced. "I don't want to grub around in dreary tunnels and risk getting stabbed in the back."

"We don't want anyone left alone," Angus said. "Just in case."

Lady Sophia heaved a dramatic sigh. "If I must. But if my satin shoes get damaged, I'll demand a new pair."

"I'll go with Ruby and Benji," I said.

That left Angus and Gregor to team up.

Gregor provided information on accessing the tunnels in the different rooms, with the entrance concealed behind tapestries or false walls, and after we received candles and torches, we got to work.

I had one advantage over the other searchers. Benji's excellent nose. If there was a hint of any strange scent in the tunnels, he'd let us know, and he wouldn't hesitate to bring down the blackguard if they were hiding.

Although the more I considered this option, the less likely it seemed. But one must keep an open mind, or clues could be missed.

We located the entrance to the easterly tunnels after shifting aside a dusty old tapestry and used gloves to heave open the creaking door. I held a candle aloft while we peered into the dense gloom.

"What do you think, Benji?" Ruby whispered. "Any rotters hiding in the shadows with a dagger, waiting to strike?"

Benji stepped forward, sniffed, and then wagged his tail.

"That's a sign all is well," I said. "We need to hurry so we can discount the mysterious madmen theory everyone is so set on. Then I can get the measure of the guests."

"Because one of them did it," Ruby stated.

"I fear so. Make haste."

We entered the cold, gloomy corridor with cobwebs hanging from the ceiling and dust tickling my nose. It was more evidence that no one had been here for some time.

"It could be Gregor." Ruby bumped into me as I slowed and cocked my head to listen intently for any hurried footsteps of someone sneaking away.

"Why pick him as the likely killer?" I asked.

"It's convenient he suddenly remembered the tunnels," she said. "Why not mention them when we were in the office after we broke through the door to reach Constance?"

"Finding a body is always a shock," I said. "We saw our fair share of casualties during the Great War, but that doesn't make us immune to the harsh reality of finding a person dead."

"We discussed how anyone got into the room when the door was locked from the inside. That should have jogged the man's memory even if he was in shock." Ruby bumped into me again and mumbled an apology. "He revealed his route into the office because he realised we'd soon be on to him, so he showed his hand and played the role of helper."

"To make himself look innocent?" I stepped over some broken stones. "Mind your step in those heels. I suppose it would look suspicious if he concealed the information until later and someone else discovered it."

"Exactly!" Ruby stumbled, and I caught her by the elbow, so she didn't fall.

"Other people in our party must know about the tunnels," I said. "Juliet, for certain, since she spent part of her childhood here. I recall her telling me that her family often spent their summers in Scotland."

"Angus would know about them," Ruby said. "As the estate manager, he'd know all the ins and outs of this place."

"He hasn't worked here all that long. Maybe he was unaware of how many there were," I said. "Juliet could have introduced Freddie to them, though."

Ruby huffed out a sigh. "That still leaves us with four suspects. It's too many!"

"We can rule out Freddie," I said. "He was in the dining room with me when Angus found Constance's body. He didn't leave the table."

We reached a turn, the cold floor uneven and numbing my toes.

Ruby prodded me on the back. "When we get out of here, you must sort this muddle."

"I'll do my best, but it won't be popular. Hearty egos dwell within these walls. Powerful ones, too."

"You must! With the police stuck and already occupied, it's up to you. And Gregor doubted the police believed him when he said someone had committed a murder. No help could be coming."

"Why can't you be in charge?"

Ruby chuckled. "I'm better with beguilement than bluntness. My skills lie in flattery. You're much more direct. A woman who gets what she needs. That's what makes us the perfect pair."

Ruby was astonishingly adept at flattery, while I marched forth, not afraid of people's opinions as I sought the truth. We were an odd combination, but we played to each other's strengths.

"I'm certain no unpleasant types are lurking in the dark," I said.

"And we know that because the killer is in our party," Ruby said.

"The sooner we find them, the better," I said on a soft but resolute sigh.

So much for a pleasant time exploring Scotland, sipping whisky, and indulging in clootie dumplings. It was time to dig out the troublemaker and ruin an old friend's special day.

Chapter 8

An hour later, we were in the castle's study along with everyone except Juliet. Most of us were dusty, with cobwebs clinging to our clothes. Lady Sophia looked pristine, so I assumed she'd left Lord Robert to search on his own while barking instructions from the doorway.

And as I suspected would happen, no one found a menacing stranger lurking in the gloom, armed and deadly.

Juliet stomped into the room. "The wretched telephone line has completely stopped working! Gregor, what did you do to it?"

Gregor's eyes widened, and he tugged at his collar.

"The defective line isn't Gregor's fault," I said. "The connection was already unstable when I spoke with Jacob before dinner."

"How are we to know if the police are even on their way?" she asked.

"They won't attempt to get through while the snow is coming down this hard." Angus stood by the window, a glass of whisky in one hand. "And if they're still looking for those hikers who had so little sense in their heads to go out in conditions like this, that will be their priority. So it should be."

Ruby stood, tugging me to my feet. "We don't need the police. Veronica has experience in matters such as this."

"I thought you worked for a newspaper in London, writing about the dead," Lady Sophia said from her seat close to the fire. "How does that make you experienced in solving a murder?"

"Veronica has a way about her," Ruby said. "She's smart, determined, and has a highly successful private investigation firm. Oh, and she also has a handsome former policeman partner."

"Who is sadly not here to assist," I murmured.

Freddie pulled a piece of cobweb from his shirt sleeve. "Juliet has said smashing things about you. But surely, solving such a dreadful crime is beyond any of us, especially a woman. You're fragile. It's a delightful quality, but it's not suitable for hunting a killer."

Angus nearly choked on his sip of whisky. He turned away and looked out of the window again, but I didn't miss his smile.

"I have the skills to extract useful information from people," I said. "I've even assisted the police a time or two when they were stuck solving a crime."

"More than that!" Ruby said. "Veronica and Benji run rings around the local force in London. They hate to admit it, but they'd be lost without her."

"Let's not go too far," I said.

"You sound like a spy." Lady Sophia's gaze was sharp. "What did you do during the war?"

I needed to breeze by that question. "Mainly admin. But the grief-stricken often have difficulty getting to the point when discussing their dearly departed. I ensure I get the pertinent information without wasting too much time. Mine or theirs."

"That sounds callous," Lady Sophia said. "I wouldn't want you to handle my family's obituaries if you approach them like that."

"The grieving have much on their minds," I replied. "They're grateful someone doesn't linger, asking pointless questions and drinking endless cups of tea while murmuring words of sympathy. And I assure you that I write top-quality obituaries."

"They're excellent quality," Ruby said. "Often humorous."

Lady Sophia lifted her chin. "How inappropriate."

"Your family would be honoured if Veronica wrote their obituaries. Her services are in high demand." Ruby's hands were clenched. "And we must use her skills to get to the heart of this problem."

"I think it's a good idea," Angus said, rejoining the conversation. "We need someone smart and efficient to deal with this muddle."

"Murder is hardly a muddle." Freddie looked a touch confused. "Shouldn't we wait until the police arrive? I'm certain they won't be long."

"With the telephone lines down and the snow threatening to consume this castle, no help is on its way," Angus said with a touch of regret in his tone. "It would be strange to have a woman investigate this crime, but it's not unheard of. I'm game if everyone else is."

Freddie turned to Juliet. "It's unbecoming, don't you think, my love?"

"Stop talking rot. I've told you all about Veronica." Juliet swatted his arm. "We should give her a chance. She's jolly well smarter than all of us put together."

Ruby's eyes sparkled with mischief. "Juliet, what exactly have you said about Veronica to Sir Frederick?"

"Oh, well, just that. She's clever. And... you know how she is," Juliet said with a hand wave. "No nonsense. Direct."

I arched an eyebrow. "There's enough waffle and prattle in society that I don't need to add to it."

"There's nothing I like more than a modern woman," Angus said, tipping me a wink. "If you can help, Veronica, then get to work. How would you like to begin?"

There were a few disgruntled mumbles from Freddie, and Lady Sophia had turned her back on the whole affair and stared into the open fire, but I pressed on.

I looked around the gathering. "I'd like to begin with my theory."

"What would that be?" Lord Robert wore a bemused expression, having roused himself from yet another nap by the fireplace, so I suspect he wasn't certain what he was asking or even where he was.

I made a quick study of everyone's face before drawing in a breath. "I believe someone in this room is the killer."

After several seconds of stunned silence, the group erupted into a cacophony of voices talking over each other.

Lord Robert, surprisingly, was the first to take a stand. "Young lady! I hope you don't include me on your list of preposterous suspects."

I inclined my head. "I discounted you since we were at the dining table together."

"As was I!" Freddie said as the voices died down.

I nodded. "Since the three of us—"

"Hold on a ticket," Lady Sophia said, addressing the room with an air of stately surety. "If we're looking at suspects, let's start with Veronica and her dining guests. It's possible you all had a hand in killing Constance, and you're working together to lie for each other."

"That's outrageous!" Freddie's cheeks were scarlet with indignation. "Why would I want Constance dead?"

"Because she spent all your money on this ridiculously bloated sham of a wedding," Lady Sophia said with a faint smirk. "I'm surprised you haven't declared the coffers empty. Juliet, remind me again how many wedding cakes you had made and then returned?"

Freddie drew himself up and tugged on the hem of his silk waistcoat. "As is proper, the bride's parents are paying for our wedding. Naturally, I offered financial support, but they're a traditional bunch, and they wouldn't hear of it."

"Even though they can't be here, my parents support our marriage." Juliet clutched Freddie's elbow. "Sophia, you say such spiteful things. It's only because you're jealous."

"Of your impressive husband-to-be? How amusing."

"At least I have a husband," Juliet snapped. "You couldn't keep yours. The society columns are still gossiping about your divorce, and it happened months ago."

Lady Sophia thumped down her glass of gin. "My personal affairs are none of your business, nor those disgusting gossip columns that masquerade as news."

"It is my business if you point the finger at my darling Freddie for being a cold-blooded killer and shove accusations towards Veronica. And Uncle Robert is the sweetest old man. None of them had anything to do with Constance's murder."

"I'm merely making a point. Veronica was quick enough to suggest I could be a killer," Lady Sophia said. "Why not repay the compliment by being just as ridiculous? You may know her, but I don't. Therefore, I'm allowed to be cautious of her intentions."

"That's enough, ladies," Angus said. "We agreed Veronica should investigate, so we need to hear her out."

"I agreed to nothing. And I'm not prepared to hear another word she says if she's suggesting I killed Constance," Lady Sophia said. "And you should know your place, Angus. You work for us, so don't tell me how to behave."

Angus pressed his lips together, but he inclined his head. "My apologies, Lady Sophia."

"You jolly well should hear everything Veronica has to say," Ruby said. "She's an ace at unpicking complicated problems."

"Several people weren't at the dinner table when Constance was stabbed." I needed to act swiftly, or the situation would spiral out of control if the group didn't think I could figure out this crime. Juliet's wedding demands had already heightened the tension, and this added complexity would make tempers snap and foolish acts occur.

"How do you know exactly when Constance died?" Lady Sophia narrowed her gaze. "You'd only know if you plunged the dagger into her back, using Freddie as your lookout and Lord Robert to cause a distraction."

"You're being absurd," Ruby said.

Benji whined softly in agreement.

"Or I paid attention to who left the dining room and at what time," I said. "I also checked Constance's pulse. Her body was warm. She died between the first course and before Angus served our next course. That leaves a space of less than twenty minutes for the killer to strike."

Another silence fell as everyone digested this unpalatable information.

"Oh, gosh. You can't think it was me," Juliet said. "I have no stomach for gruesome deeds. And having scoffed my entire first course and half of Freddie's, I wouldn't have kept my food down if I'd undertaken anything so distressing and vigorous."

"You have had a delicate constitution recently, my love." Freddie patted Juliet's hand. "I'm willing to hear what Veronica has to say. What do you think happened to Constance?"

I nodded my thanks at another voice of assent. "That's to be discovered. I'd appreciate you answering the same questions so we can learn the motive for her death. I'll speak with you all separately."

"Surely that's unnecessary," Freddie protested. "We can do it here and move on."

"It will ensure the information doesn't become confused," I said. "It's easy to influence another person, especially when you have a strong character."

"Ah, say no more." Freddie drew back his shoulders, having decided I meant him. "I've been told I'm ruthless at the negotiation table. Darling, are you feeling strong enough to face Veronica's questions alone? I'm certain she'll be kind to you."

Juliet's expression fell. "I... I can't be a suspect."

"It would be unfair of me not to question you because we have a friendship," I said.

"Yes, we do! An excellent one. You know my character, which means you know I'm innocent."

"Then this won't take long, will it?" I said. "Let's get this over with and start with you."

After several theatrical huffs and more words of comfort from Freddie, Juliet stomped out of the room.

"If the blushing bride wasn't miserable before this murder, she soon will be," Ruby whispered to me.

"I'll deal with Juliet," I murmured. "You stay here with Benji and watch for suspicious behaviour."

Ruby's eyes widened, but she nodded. "Good luck."

I would need it if I were to maintain this friendship with Juliet while suggesting she was the killer.

Chapter 9

The storm clawed at the ancient walls of the castle as I closed the drawing room door behind me. Snow hissed against the windows, turning the world beyond into a white oblivion. Only the fire's low crackle and the tick of the long-case clock served as a source of comfort.

Juliet had stopped by the fire. Her red gown shimmered in the light, but the tremor in her hands betrayed her nerves. She clutched a lace handkerchief.

"Must we do this, Ronnie?" she asked, her childhood nickname for me softening the plea. "You know I'm honest. Surely you don't suspect me."

I moved closer. "That is exactly why we must speak privately. Friendship deserves honesty, not polite evasions to avoid group gossip. You must understand."

She swallowed and glanced towards the door. "Freddie will worry. He enjoys a good worry, the poor dear. I fear he's lost hair since I began the wedding plans. Who knew it would grow to be so grand?"

"He knows I need your statement. Sit down, Juliet. There's nothing to concern yourself with. I must show fairness, or any information I uncover will be of no value to the police."

The velvet armchair sighed as she obeyed, and I settled opposite.

"Let's start at the beginning," I said. "When did you first meet Constance?"

Juliet clasped the handkerchief tighter. "In October. Just over two years ago. I interviewed a dozen society hostesses before settling on her."

"Why choose Constance over the other hostesses?" I asked.

"She came highly recommended, and when we met, she had a calm manner. Nothing flustered her. I thought that would be important, given how lavish my plans are." Her voice softened. "Constance even joked she could herd swans if I insisted, and I was considering having birds at the wedding, but lovebirds. Although swans would be wonderful. Perhaps it's not too late... oh, what am I saying? It's too late for any changes now."

I allowed myself a small smile. Juliet had always had a fanciful imagination. "Did you and Constance ever quarrel?"

"Of course not," she said swiftly. "Nothing was ever too much trouble."

"There were no disagreements at all? If you'll forgive me for saying, it is all so extravagant and must have been tricky to put together."

"You cannot put a price on good taste." Juliet sniffed delicately. "This is to be my only wedding, so I must ensure it is perfection. You see that, don't you? I know you aren't the wedding sort, but this matters to me. It matters to a lot of people."

"I understand. Does that mean there was no disharmony between you?" I pressed.

Juliet lowered her gaze to the rose-patterned carpet. "Nothing worth mentioning."

The clock ticked louder in the pause that followed. I let it stretch, hoping silence would coax a fissure in Juliet's composure.

"Tell me about this evening," I said at last. "You left the dining room just after the first course was cleared."

Her head lifted. "I wanted to ensure all was well in the kitchen. Angus is a dear fellow, but we didn't employ him to provide the catering. Although it went clear out of my head who would serve our meal, so I'm glad he took charge."

"Did you go anywhere else?"

"I popped to my bedroom."

"For how long?" I asked.

Juliet's eyes flickered towards the window, where the storm scratched like a persistent caller. "Perhaps three minutes. I retouched my lipstick. I must ensure Freddie continues to see me as perfection."

"Did anyone see you?"

"No. Everyone was at the table, or so I thought." Juliet sighed. "What a terrible bind we find ourselves in."

"You didn't see Constance?" I asked.

"Why would I?"

"Perhaps to discuss your thoughts on the meal."

"No. I didn't see her."

"Take a moment. Are you certain you didn't glimpse her heading towards the Thistle Inn?"

The firelight danced across Juliet's face, catching the faintest flush in her cheeks. "I didn't see Constance when I left the table, but my focus was elsewhere. When it comes time for you to marry Jacob, you'll understand why everything else becomes insignificant."

"I'm sure I will," I murmured. "Constance appeared tired. Could it have been because of your demands?"

Juliet's hand jerked, crushing the handkerchief into a ball. "Demands for perfection. Constance thought the flowers might not survive the cold, but I assured her she didn't know what she was talking about. And she had yet to resolve the colour error."

"Did you argue about that?"

"I am her employer, so she does what I tell her. Well, at least she did. Constance was well-mannered and caused no trouble."

"And yet she ended the night stabbed in a locked office, so she must have troubled someone."

Juliet flinched. "Don't say it so plainly. It makes you sound cold. Constance was a sweet girl."

"She was also a shrewd businesswoman and well-known in high society circles as a person who successfully managed many high-profile events," I replied. "And she must have kept meticulous notes. Suppose she discovered something she thought unwise to proceed with?"

"Like what?"

"That is what I'm asking you."

Juliet's chin lifted. "Ronnie, really. I invited you here to stand beside me on my happiest day, not to accuse me of scandal."

"I'm not accusing," I said softly. "I'm observing. You left the table, went to the kitchen and then to your room. In that same window of time, Constance was killed. The police would be interested in this pattern of movement for the same reason I am."

Juliet's fingers were white-knuckled on the handkerchief, and I remembered our Sunday school Bible study debates where she'd tried to win by charm then by yelling. Juliet had a temper.

"Do you believe I could drive a knife into someone's back?" she asked, her voice thin.

"I believe anyone is capable of anything when sufficiently provoked or scared."

Juliet's breath hitched. "You can't think me capable of such a thing."

I let her unravel a little as I reached forward and squeezed her hand. Sympathy was a tool as useful as any question when a person had something to hide. It encouraged them to pour out what their pride would not.

"I sincerely hope you didn't." I'd yet to discover a suitably fierce motive, but with no alibi, I couldn't discount her. "Did Constance have any concern for her welfare?"

Juliet's pale forehead wrinkled. "She mentioned nothing to me. Although..."

"Go on."

"I saw her with someone. Or perhaps I didn't. This castle plays tricks with the shadows." "What do you think you saw?" I asked. "Describe the shadow."

"It was a tall person in a long coat. A man's silhouette. I thought it was Freddie at first." Shame flushed Juliet's face. "I'll admit to a touch of jealousy. After all, he's such a catch. But his gait differed from this fellow's. The shadow paused at the oak door by the study, and Constance passed him. They exchanged words. I couldn't hear them. Then she moved on."

"Did Constance seem anxious after that exchange?" I asked.

"We spoke only of the wedding." Juliet paused. "But after that, she seemed keen for things to conclude here."

"Constance had another event to arrange?"

"I expect so, although I never asked." Juliet bit her bottom lip. "There was mention, and only the briefest of mentions, of her stepping aside and another hostess completing the wedding. I laughed it off. That wasn't a serious suggestion, given how close we are to the happiest day of my life."

"Constance threatened to resign? If she'd left, your wedding would have been delayed."

"She didn't mean it!" Juliet looked away. "I'm sure of it. Who wouldn't want this extraordinary event on their work record? She'd have had her pick of jobs after this."

I sat back. If Constance had left, it would have spoiled more than the wedding. The gossip about Juliet and Freddie's ruined day would spread like a pox through a medieval village. To have one's special day tarnished might be unforgivable, especially when it had been two years in the making.

"Who do you think benefits most from Constance's death?" I asked.

Juliet didn't answer immediately. "I don't know. But it wasn't me. And I'm certain it was no one here."

"You still wish to pursue the lurking stranger idea?"

"It is more than an idea! It must be the truth. It's the only thing that makes sense."

For a moment, we sat in the firelight, two women in a world that had turned thin and sharp, the clock ticking like a judge.

"Thank you," I said, rising from my seat. "I will speak to the rest of the party, and we'll sort this out."

Juliet tried to stand and swayed. I caught her arm to steady her.

"You must tell me you believe me." She gripped my hand.

I held her gaze, and with that small cruelty friendship permits when truths must be prised from the heart, I told it plain. "I believe you are frightened, Juliet. I don't yet know if I believe you are innocent, but I will find out the truth."

She let out a sound that wasn't quite a sob and not quite a laugh. "You have a way with words. I always considered you terribly clever when we were children. I still do. What would you like me to do now?"

"Try not to worry too much. And please send in Freddie."

Juliet opened her mouth then pressed her lips together. "I ask only one thing. Whatever you do, don't spoil my wedding day."

I waited until the door closed before sighing. Surely Juliet must see that a murder had quite efficiently achieved that task.

Chapter 10

The door creaked open, and I looked up to find Ruby slipping into the room. Beside her, Benji padded in, his ears twitching as the wind gave another icy howl beyond the stone.

"I come bearing smuggled biscuits," Ruby said, holding up a folded napkin. "I thought you'd appreciate a treat."

"I need a great deal more than biscuits, but they're welcome."

Benji gave a soft woof and pressed his head against my thigh. I reached down and scratched behind his ears. His presence was always soothing.

"How did Juliet hold up under questioning?" Ruby settled beside the fire and unwrapped her napkin to reveal two crumbling shortbreads.

"She's nervous," I said. "And a touch dramatic. She's still convinced the wedding will go ahead."

Ruby broke a biscuit in half and handed me a piece. "I remember you telling me she pretended to faint when summoned to read from the Gospel of St Luke because she couldn't pronounce the longer words."

I took the biscuit and smiled. "Yes, and she'd even practised the fall to create the biggest shock."

We lapsed into a companionable silence, watching the fire stretch and twist in the grate. Benji curled beside my feet.

After a moment, Ruby leaned in. "Everyone is nervous."

"No doubt with a killer among us."

"That's just it. The killer really could be outside!"

"Whatever makes you say that?"

"Just before I came in here, a sound came from the grounds, close to the castle."

"Was it an animal?" I asked.

"It sounded like footsteps, slow and deliberate crunching through the snow."

My stomach tightened. "Who heard them?"

"All of us! And Lady Sophia swore she saw something move past the window. Everyone got up and rushed to look. It was chaotic. I got knocked out of the way by Lord Robert, although I think that was a ruse, so he had an excuse to grab me."

"What did you see when you got to the window?"

"It took me a minute to push to the front, but Lord Robert said it was a man in a dark coat. Freddie swore he saw tracks, but I couldn't see them. I suppose the snow covered them. Lady Sophia made a comment about Constance's ghost returning to haunt us, but I could tell she was shaken."

"That was tactless of her, but hardly surprising, given her taciturn nature." I raised an eyebrow. "Besides, ghosts don't leave footprints."

"Murderers do," Ruby said. "Perhaps there is a person unaccounted for, and we've been hasty in thinking it was someone in the castle."

There was a pause as the fire snapped sharply, its light flaring across the carpet.

"If there is someone out there, they've truly lost their senses to remain outside on such a bitter night," I said. "Perhaps it was nothing, and nerves got the better of our party."

"But I heard something!" Ruby said. "And I'm not nervous. I don't have to worry about you thinking me a killer."

"Well, you don't have an alibi."

Ruby swatted my arm. "How dare you!"

I chuckled. "In all seriousness, if someone is using the storm to move around unseen, they may not be finished yet."

Ruby gave a small nod. "It rattled everyone. Even Freddie looked pale. Well, paler than usual. Angus bolted to the main doors and checked the locks twice. And Lord Robert stood holding a decanter of port like a weapon."

"Perhaps a heightened sense of urgency will help me figure this out. People will be more willing to share if they consider themselves vulnerable." I brushed biscuit crumbs from my dress, which Benji happily consumed.

Ruby finished her last bite of shortbread. "They're not just wondering who killed Constance. They're wondering who might be next. I'll keep my eyes open and report back if I see anyone outside."

"And I shall continue the questioning."

Ruby stood and hurried to the door. She inched it open, then looked back at me. "Freddie's lurking outside. Shall I tell him you'll be gentle?"

"You may do so, but that would be untrue."

"And that's why you'll solve this." Ruby grinned and then slipped out.

I called in Freddie.

His smile was tight as he closed the door behind him. "I hear it's my turn to be questioned."

"Indeed. Do take a seat."

He crossed to the fire and extended his hands towards the flames. "It's a hellish night for it."

"Murder makes any evening hellish."

Freddie didn't respond. The light from the fire cast shifting lines across his face.

"This won't take long," I said. "Please sit."

Freddie arched a brow but did as he was told. "I have theories on what happened."

I raised an eyebrow. "Do you? Please, I'm open to suggestions."

He glanced briefly towards the window, where the storm still raged. "I don't think it was one of us."

"You mean one of the wedding party?"

"I mean not anyone inside the castle." Freddie leaned forward, his elbows resting on his knees. "This place is remote and difficult to reach even in fair weather. Now we're stranded in the middle of a snowstorm, cut off from the nearest village by miles of impassable roads, and with no way to telephone for help."

"Making it difficult for anyone to get in or out," I said.

"Exactly." He looked at me steadily. "Which is why someone must have arrived before the snow started. They hid nearby and waited. This pile of bricks is huge, so there are plenty of rooms to conceal oneself and wait for the perfect moment. And there are old buildings on the grounds that would conceal an entire platoon."

"You think a stranger watched Constance break from the group during the evening and went after her?"

"Indeed, I do!" Freddie said. "Constance was private. Professional, yes, but guarded, and she always had a reason to step away. That kind of habit makes someone vulnerable."

"So she was stabbed because she was the easiest target?"

"There can be no other reason." His voice was calm, but there was tension in it. "This castle has too many entrances. Too many places to hide. And the storm masks movement and sounds. We are all vulnerable."

"It seems unlikely a stranger would travel out this far simply to kill. There must be a motive. After all, there are easier places to reach in this area."

"Ah. Well, perhaps you have a point, but that makes it even more unnerving. If Constance was killed because of something personal, then we don't understand what danger we're in. This could be about her, and only her... or it could be about something more." Freddie shifted in his seat.

Outside, a dull crash echoed through the stone, perhaps a shutter breaking loose or snow cascading from the roof. Freddie didn't flinch, but his eyes tracked the sound.

"What about the movement you all saw outside?" I asked. "That lends weight to your theory."

"Perhaps." Freddie's jaw shifted slightly. "I saw... something. I'm unsure what it was."

"Describe it, please."

He hesitated then shook his head. "The storm plays tricks with the eyes. As soon as someone said it was a person, that's all I could see. But now I don't know."

"It fits your theory of an unhinged individual stalking us."

Freddie rubbed his forehead. "I don't know what to believe. Every option feels less salubrious."

If Freddie wished to divert attention from himself, he should have clung to the theory of the stranger. Instead, he was talking himself out of the possibility.

"Let's come back to Constance," I said.

"Yes. Of course."

"What was your opinion of her?"

"Constance was efficient. Disciplined. She kept things moving with the wedding plans." Freddie paused. "We didn't speak often, but when we did, she was polite. I had the impression she didn't care much for me, though."

"Why do you say that?"

Freddie offered a half-smile. "Constance liked to be in charge. I like order. Occasionally, those ideals clashed."

"Did you argue?"

"Not directly. But Constance would often bypass me and speak with Juliet, even on matters I should have approved. I let some things pass. I didn't see the point in challenging her over flower arrangements and seating charts. Those are women's proclivities. But the wedding includes me, so I would have appreciated some say in matters."

That was a small motive, but not a strong enough one to commit a murder.

"Did Constance ever threaten to leave your service and not complete her work?"

"Juliet mentioned a difficult conversation," Freddie said. "But I assumed Constance was tired and wouldn't go through with it. This wedding will be one of a kind, so no detail can be overlooked."

"Did you want her gone?"

"No." He met my gaze squarely. "But I wasn't sorry when Constance said she might leave. I thought a more respectful replacement might suit everyone. Besides, I was never set on a winter wedding, so if there had been a short delay while we'd found someone else, I wouldn't have minded."

A pause stretched between us. Freddie's eyes widened, and he reached out as if to take my hand but stopped himself.

"That's not a motive!"

"Perhaps not," I replied. "But you've admitted you had something to gain by Constance being dead."

Freddie sat forward, colour rising beneath the fine bones of his cheeks. "You're twisting my words. I had no quarrel with Constance. We may have disagreed on tone, but not substance. I had no reason to harm her."

"You'd be surprised what people will do when someone gets in their way."

He stood abruptly. "This is madness! We're wasting time looking inward when it's obvious there's someone else involved. A deranged stranger." He jabbed a finger at the window.

"We're back to that idea? It would be convenient." I tilted my head. "Especially when the internal motives touch a little too close to home."

Freddie turned back, lips parted to argue, but then something flickered in his gaze. "My dear Veronica, don't tell me you've forgotten that I was at the table with you."

"I'm aware."

He clapped his hands together. "Then you're my alibi! All of this has been for nothing."

I bit back a sigh. "You're correct. You didn't leave the table during the window in which Constance died."

Freddie exhaled sharply then laughed. "Thank God. You were testing me! Juliet was right about you."

"What was she right about?"

"Oh, well, she mentioned a few things. Your sharp mind was one topic of conversation."

"And my sharp tongue, perhaps?"

His cheeks flushed even more. "I don't remember everything we discussed. All that matters is you know I'm an innocent man."

"Don't get too comfortable," I said. "An alibi simply means you didn't wield the knife, not that you didn't have reason to want it done."

He blinked. "What in the devil are you suggesting? That I arranged for Constance to be killed?"

"I'm suggesting I have ruled nothing out until we have a confession."

A silence passed between us. The fire hissed as a gust of wind swept across the chimney.

"I see," Freddie said finally. "Well then, I shall leave you and your unfounded theorising, Miss Vale." With that, he turned and left, closing the door behind him with more force than necessary.

I leaned back in the chair. Why was Freddie so certain it was no one inside the castle? Did he know something about a person that made him feel he had to conceal information? Could it be someone close to him who was involved? A fiancée, perhaps?

It was time for a new suspect.

Chapter 11

Lord Robert Augustine settled into the armchair with a long sigh and patted around his waistcoat. He looked up as though expecting a valet to appear from the shadows and locate whatever it was he was looking for.

When no help arrived, his gaze settled on me. "Be a good girl and fetch my pipe and slippers, would you?" He waved a liver-spotted hand in the vague direction of the fireplace. "And perhaps a brandy. All this murder business is dashed exhausting."

I didn't move. "You've mistaken me for a servant, Lord Robert."

He blinked at me, momentarily disoriented, whether from my bluntness or whatever pills he rattled into his system daily, I couldn't tell. Then he gave a raspy chuckle and settled deeper into the chair.

"That's a tart tongue you have, Miss Vale. You'll frighten off any suitors if you don't soften yourself."

"Then it's a good thing I'm here to solve a murder and not arrange my marriage."

He harrumphed. "Well, let's get on with it then. I suppose you want to know if I plunged the knife in myself, do you?"

"Let's begin with something simpler. How did you know Constance?" I asked.

"I did not know her," he said. "And before we start with these parlour games, I must ask about your delightful friend."

"You're referring to Ruby?"

"Yes, that's the one." Lord Robert gave a lecherous little smile that set my teeth on edge. "She's not what I'd expect of a war widow. A bit too polished. Lovely frocks. And a fine pair of legs."

I stared at him in silence.

"She makes the effort," he continued, clearly mistaking my silence for an invitation to continue his inappropriate conversation. "Most widows let themselves fade. Hair pinned like a governess, drab dresses, faces like vinegar. But Ruby still knows how to turn a head."

"She doesn't dress for your approval," I said coolly.

"Oh, don't be so sure about that," he said with a chuckle. "There's a difference between grief and performance. Some women make mourning a profession."

"She lost her husband in the war!" The lie slid ever more easily from my tongue the more I said it. I didn't enjoy concealment, but Ruby's reputation was at stake, and I would do anything to protect her.

"Many women did," Lord Robert said. "But most of them aren't quite so... vivid about it. Still, perhaps she's cleverer than she looks and knows how to keep the attention of a certain class of man. It wouldn't be the first girl to use loss as a calling card to gain access to a soft heart and a large income."

I gripped the edge of the seat. "Are we finished with your thoughts on women's wardrobes and motivations for capturing men?"

He raised his brows, pleased with himself. "I suppose I've struck a nerve. You unmarried girls are all the same. There's no need to be so prim."

"No, Lord Robert. Not prim. But you've simply reminded me that some men grow old without ever growing up."

He smirked but didn't reply. "I expect your friend will find me in her own time and suggest an association. Perhaps we will see much more of each other in the near future. Won't that be pleasant?"

"Shall we proceed with the matter at hand?" I asked.

Lord Robert shrugged. "By all means. I enjoy a good diversion. You're not as handsome as your companion, but I see fire in those eyes."

Fire I would blast at him if he kept being so rude. "Returning to Constance, tell me of your association with her."

"There was no association."

"You didn't speak to her at all? Not even to bark an order?"

"I don't involve myself in the domestic squabbles of weddings. I was told when to appear and where to sit. That was quite enough involvement, thank you."

"You're a member of the family. I find it difficult to believe you had no interaction with the woman organising the entire event. An event that will be the talk of society circles for many weeks."

He sniffed. "She was a high society hostess, not a duchess. I don't make a habit of engaging with the help."

From the way he leered at any woman, I didn't believe that.

"I'm at a loss as to why you must speak with me, Miss Vale," Lord Robert continued. "You were next to me at the dining table while this business occurred."

"Yes, I recall you napping through most of the first course."

"As if I'd do such a thing. Although my new pills make me tired. But that is beside the point."

"People have paid others to commit murder," I said. "You have wealth. Influence. Will you, hand on heart, tell me you've never paid someone else to do your dirty work?"

Lord Robert's gaze flicked to the fireplace. "I don't like what you're implying." He fussed with the hem of his sleeve as though it might provide protection.

I waited a beat. Then two more.

"Oh, very well." Lord Robert gave a dry bark of laughter. "What aristocrat hasn't been a rogue in his time?"

"Is that a confession?"

"It's a reality," he snapped. "Men in my position solve problems quickly and efficiently. That doesn't make them murderers."

"But it makes them capable of paying others to commit such a crime."

Lord Robert narrowed his eyes. "Are you suggesting I hired someone to kill our society hostess? What would I possibly have to gain from that act of senseless violence?"

"That's what I'm determining." I met his gaze evenly. "You are a member of this family, so you must have been interested in how much this wedding was costing."

"I have no care of such trivial matters, and I don't talk to commoners about money."

I ignored his slight. "Juliet wanted the best of everything. Did you think she was taking matters too far? Did you mention it to Constance and ask her to reduce the expenditure?"

"This wedding is of little interest to me, and I'm not paying for it," Lord Robert said. "I'm here because others expected me to be. With Juliet's parents absent, someone had to represent the elder members of the family. That duty fell on my shoulders, and I accepted it, but that is as far as it goes."

"Constance was meticulous. She wouldn't have taken kindly to being told to trim the budget for a wedding that would have been the making of her career."

"If she were that precious, it's a wonder she lasted this long in the business. But as I said, I never dealt with her directly. And women shouldn't focus on their careers but on ensuring their husbands are happy and their homes run efficiently." Lord Robert slapped a hand against the arm of his chair. "This blasted war has a lot to answer for."

"I find it hard to believe a man as proud as you would sit quietly while a woman of no rank orchestrated an event in your ancestral home," I said as sweetly as my simmering rage allowed.

"This isn't my ancestral home," he snapped. "It belongs to my brother and will be passed to his children. If it were mine..." he flashed a glare at me.

I smiled thinly. "So, you do disapprove of some things."

He huffed, the sound thick with disdain. "I disapprove of fuss. I disapprove of modern weddings, and vulgar entertainment, and anyone of a lowly rank telling me what to do. That includes you, Miss Vale."

"And Constance?"

"I told you, I didn't know the woman." A vein throbbed in his forehead.

"What if Constance had threatened to walk away at a crucial time in the wedding preparations?" I asked.

"I expect Juliet would have found someone else to tie her ribbons and fluff her veil," Lord Robert said dryly. "You're reaching, Miss Vale. I was at the dining table with you. My hands are clean."

"If you're keeping something from me," I said softly, "now is the time to reveal all."

"I have nothing to reveal. Not to the likes of you," he snapped. "I came here to play the part of the family patriarch and do my duty, not to be accused of murder."

"No one is accusing you," I said. "Not yet."

Lord Robert's eyes were clear and cold. "You ought to tread carefully, Miss Vale. You're not as untouchable as your confidence belies."

"Neither are you." I stood, and he did the same. "We're in the same castle, Lord Robert, and the doors are all locked. No one gets in, and no one leaves until we find the killer."

For a moment, we stared at one another, two figures framed by firelight, each as unmoved as the other.

His lip curled faintly. "You've got a talent for poking around in matters that don't concern you. You should be careful with that."

"And you should remind yourself that you're not above suspicion because you have a title."

Lord Robert grunted. Half amusement, half contempt. "You think being clever makes you dangerous. It doesn't. It makes you tiresome. Men, in particular, must find your company most disagreeable."

"I have no quibbles with being disagreeable if it winkles out people's foul secrets." I leaned closer. "What secrets of yours lurk in the shadows?"

He gripped the back of the chair with long, bony fingers. "I've dealt with war, scandal, Parliament, and women twice as fierce as you. If I have anything worth hiding, it will remain hidden until I decide otherwise."

"Let's hope you're right," I said. "Otherwise, we'll be having this conversation again, with a police officer present."

Lord Robert stepped away. "Playing detective doesn't suit you."

"I'm not playing," I said quietly. "And I will find out who murdered Constance."

He looked me over, his eyes narrowed. Then he turned, muttering something beneath his breath, something I didn't quite catch but suspected wasn't complimentary, and made his way towards the door with the gait of a man who felt old age deep in his bones.

Lord Robert paused with one hand on the door. "For what it's worth, I didn't kill Constance. But whoever did it must have had a good reason." The door closed behind him with a soft click.

There was never a good reason to kill. I remained standing for a moment, my eyes on the fire, listening to the wind throw itself against the castle walls.

Outside, a thick, white blanket of frigidness buried everything. And inside, much to my frustration, the truth remained stubbornly buried, too.

Chapter 12

The vestibule was cold enough to freeze a thought, but I didn't care. I needed a bite of cold air to refresh myself after dealing with Lord Robert and his lecherous predilections.

I stood just inside the inner door, wrapped in my coat, my cheeks tingling as the air bit at them. Although the outer door remained locked, gaps in the wood made the temperature feel like an icebox.

Benji pressed against my leg, his warm body a comfort. I rested a hand on his head, grateful for the quiet to gather myself.

Ruby appeared a second later, slipping out from the hallway with a grin and a bright blue scarf wrapped around her neck.

"There you are!" She blew into her hands. "I thought Lord Robert and his charming manners had convinced you into a dark corner."

"If he'd lured me outside, I'd have shoved him into a snowdrift and buried him," I said. "The man is an obnoxious boar. And I mean the hairy pig variety, not the slack-jawed toff variety."

She chuckled. "When he returned to the room, he was fuming, although he still had time to comment on my pleasing ankles as if I were a Victorian scandal flashing too much flesh."

"Consider this your official warning," I said. "Lord Robert has taken an interest in you, and he expects you to reciprocate."

Her face contorted. "Good Lord! I'd rather court a toad. One with warts and a throat that expands to an obnoxiously colossal size before it croaks."

I smiled despite myself. "He thinks you're falsifying your grief for attention so a sympathetic man of means pities you and claims you as his mistress."

"Well, that's rich," Ruby muttered.

"That's the root of this issue. Lord Robert is immensely wealthy, titled, and grossly *entitled* as a result."

"He's old enough to be my grandfather!"

"But he's not so frail, despite his stiff joints when he sits for too long. Ensure you never find yourself alone with him."

She gave an indelicate snort. "Lord Robert may have a title, but I still know where his family jewels are. My knee will effectively connect with them if he does more than make inappropriate comments about my ankles."

Benji gave a soft bark, as if in agreement.

"How are the remaining suspects dealing with the wait?" I asked.

"Everyone's still on edge." Ruby glanced down the hall. "Freddie's taken up residence in the billiards room. Juliet's redoing the seating plan again, much to Lady

Sophia's ridicule. Gregor and Angus are huddled over a decanter of port, muttering to themselves."

"Can you hear what they're discussing?"

"It's nothing dubious. They're worried about the weather and how soon the police will arrive."

"Interesting. Perhaps because they need to conceal evidence?"

"Don't say that. I like Angus. I hope he isn't involved."

"Focus on the task at hand and not the handsome Scotsman in the kilt."

"Oh! You think he's handsome, too?"

"Enough of that!" I smiled at her. "Any more sightings of the mysterious person outside?"

"A lot of whispering, but no one agrees about what it was," Ruby said. "I'll keep watching. Anyway, your break time is over. You've got Lady Sophia next."

I groaned softly. "Must I? Her tongue is so sharp."

"Almost as sharp as yours." Ruby squeezed my arm. "She'll be no match for you."

"I do hope you're right. You'd better send her in."

"Brace yourself." Ruby disappeared along the hall.

Benji looked up at me. I looked down at him.

"Come on, boy. Let's go deal with this lady and see how she behaves under scrutiny."

We returned to the room just in time to hear the swish of silk. Lady Sophia entered as though she were being announced at a coming-out ball, trailing the scent of expensive perfume.

"Miss Vale." She fanned her fingers as though the air were offensive. "I hope we can get this business over with quickly."

I gestured to the chair Lord Robert had vacated. "I'll try not to keep you long."

She sat with a practised elegance, the hem of her dress just brushing the floor.

Benji sat beside me, alert.

"You know why I need to speak with you," I began.

"We've been whispering about little else," Lady Sophia said with a hint of boredom in her voice. "A society hostess stabbed in a locked room? Such a scandal. How will poor Juliet deal with this tragedy when all eyes were meant to be focused on her becoming Lady Galton the Third?"

"With responsibility and great care," I said. "As should you, since this murder will affect all of you."

"I care little for gossip. Proceed with whatever it is you do in matters such as this."

I liked a woman who got straight to the heart of the matter. "You left the table after the first course was over. Where did you go?"

"To my room. I had a headache."

"Did anyone see you?"

"No. And I wasn't aware I needed an escort to powder my nose."

I paused. "Were you angry with Constance?"

Lady Sophia rolled her eyes. "Don't be ridiculous. I didn't think about Constance long enough to form any emotion. She was hired help, ensuring this wedding would be as ridiculous as Juliet desired it to be."

"That suggests you don't enjoy weddings. All weddings or just this one?"

"I think it's absurd. Juliet has constructed a fantasy out of silk and florists and is sprinting towards it with all the insight of a giddy schoolgirl. She should show decorum. She said it would be the best day of her life. That her life would be complete once married." Lady Sophia gave a dry laugh. "If Juliet truly believes that, then I almost pity her."

"You've been married."

Her posture stiffened. "And what of it?"

"You understand how trying these things can be. And you must also understand some women consider marriage to be of the utmost importance."

"Trying?" Lady Sophia echoed, her lips tightening. "Trying is dropping your husband's name from your invitation cards and pretending it was your idea."

"The divorce wasn't at your instigation?"

"That is none of your business." Icicles could have formed around the coldness in Lady Sophia's tone. "Have you spoken to Freddie?"

"You know I have."

"Perhaps you asked the wrong questions. Men like that don't stay faithful for long. Juliet may be planning a fairy tale, but our dear Frederick looks like he's ready to rewrite it."

"I've seen no evidence of that."

"Then you haven't been watching as closely as you should have. Freddie and Constance had their moments."

"Moments? Are you suggesting they were involved?" I asked.

Lady Sophia tilted her head while studying an oil painting on the wall. "Involved is such a heavy word. Let's just say they shared a certain fondness. A mutual understanding."

"You're being vague. Why?"

"Because vague is all I have." Her eyes slid lazily back to mine. "They weren't caught kissing in the conservatory, if that's what you're hoping. But they often lingered in conversation. And Freddie laughed more freely with her than he ever does with Juliet. Constance was the sort who noticed when a man's tie was crooked. She fixed his collar at least twice yesterday. Intimate gestures in plain sight are so revealing. Don't you think?"

"Or they're professional gestures to ensure her client looks his best," I offered.

Lady Sophia gently snorted. "A pretty woman touches a man like that when she knows he could set her up as his mistress and give her everything she desires."

I didn't respond.

"You don't believe me?" she asked.

"I notice patterns. And when someone tries to divert attention from themselves, I ask why."

Lady Sophia leaned forward slightly. "I've said nothing that isn't common knowledge."

"Did Juliet notice this shared fondness between Freddie and Constance?"

Lady Sophia's smile deepened. "If she did, she buried it. That girl has built her life like a wedding cake. Layers and icing and sugar flowers that will swiftly decay. She won't let anything knock it over. Not even reality."

"And what about you?" I asked. "Why point me towards Freddie?"

Lady Sophia sat back again, smoothing her dress. "Because Juliet will never believe it if it comes from me. But you? She might listen to you. After all, you're such splendid friends."

"That almost sounds generous, and from what I've learned of you, you're never generous," I said.

"Don't mistake honesty for generosity. I simply prefer the truth to hypocrisy."

Lady Sophia was clever, and I'd yet to decide if this was a distraction or a diversion towards the killer.

"Did you speak to Constance before she died?" I asked.

She lifted one shoulder in an elegant shrug. "Briefly. In the corridor outside the drawing room. She looked tired. I told her she should demand extra pay for the special attention she was giving Freddie."

"And what did Constance say?"

Lady Sophia hesitated. "She blushed and said she'd manage and she'd be gone soon anyway."

"Gone where?"

"I assumed she meant home. How should I know?"

"You didn't ask?"

"Why would I?"

"Didn't it strike you as strange?"

"Everything in this castle strikes me as strange. The bizarre wedding, most of all." Lady Sophia rose from her seat. "I can furnish you with nothing else helpful. You have questioned my whereabouts, and I have offered you an entirely plausible suspect. What more do you want from me?"

"What about the person you saw outside?" I asked.

Lady Sophia's gaze drifted to the window. "Little disturbs me, but this death has. I didn't know or like Constance. Neither did I dislike her. She was just there, always in the background, like a shadow. Now, that shadow is gone."

"And…" I prompted.

"When one's countenance is rattled, it may cause you to see things that aren't there."

"You imagined seeing someone in the snow?"

"I… am less sure than I was. That is all I can say." She moved towards the door. "Although I will say this. You're clever, Miss Vale, but not as clever as you think. And poking around in private matters won't make you popular. And popularity, whether you admit it, is a currency a woman like you can't afford to squander."

"I'm not here to be liked."

"No, you're here to be right. And that too can be costly."

I met her gaze with unwavering certainty. "Truth usually is, especially when it uncovers a secret you don't want revealed."

Lady Sophia paused by the door just long enough to add, "Be careful, Miss Vale. You're interfering with a family that has been the backbone of this country for hundreds of years. We'll be remembered long after your tedious little obituaries have turned to dust." With that cutting remark, she swept out of the room.

"There is nothing tedious about my obituaries," I muttered.

Benji shifted at my feet and gave a small, disgruntled huff.

I stared at the closed door. Lady Sophia had given me no checkable alibi, a veiled accusation against Freddie that came with no proof other than her own observations, and a warning to mind my own business. That was more than enough to keep her near the centre of the suspect web.

Chapter 13

Rather than summoning the next suspect, I walked down the hallway and found Angus in the small sitting room off the library, inspecting the decanters sitting neatly on a drinks trolley. He looked more ready to offer me a dram of whisky and have a friendly conversation than be questioned in a murder investigation.

"Miss Vale," he said warmly when he saw me in the doorway. "You'll be wantin' to talk to me now, then? Shall we go to your interrogation room, or is here a fine enough place for your needs?"

"Here will be fine."

"I'm glad. This is one of my favourite rooms in the castle. I prefer smaller spaces. They're easier to keep warm." Angus gestured to the trolley. "Would you be in the mood for something from this collection? I'd say there's something here for everyone's taste."

"Thank you. Not at this time," I said.

"Do you mind if I do?"

"Provided the Augustine family has no issue with you helping yourself, then I can hardly object."

Angus smiled as he poured a measure of rich amber liquid into a glass. "I'd say they've got more on their minds than the decanters looking low."

I settled into a chair and gestured to the seat opposite mine.

Angus lowered himself into the seat with a quiet grunt. "How's the sleuthing going?"

"I'm just fact gathering, so far."

"I'd say it's a wee bit more than that."

"Why would you think so?" I asked.

"Ruby has been telling me all about your experience."

I arched an eyebrow. "I'm sure she has."

He grinned. "She's great fun. And that bairn of hers is adorable."

"Grace has a certain appeal, especially when she's content," I said. "Now, you've been the castle manager for how long?"

"Two years," Angus said, remaining at ease as I began my questioning. "I started as a groundsman on a different estate to the west of Scotland and moved up over the years. When the old castle steward retired from Augustine Castle, I saw an opportunity to set my stall."

"And you were helping Constance with the upcoming wedding arrangements?"

"Aye. I did what I could. This isn't the first wedding we've hosted here," Angus said. "Family friends have enjoyed the setting over the years."

"What was your opinion of Constance?" I asked.

"She was a polite lady and worked hard." Angus sipped his drink. "I wondered if it was something she enjoyed, though. Constance didn't smile often, but weddings don't always bring out the best in people."

"They certainly aren't my favourite social event."

Angus smiled broadly. "I'd gathered as much."

"On the night Constance died, you didn't join us at dinner."

He shook his head. "No, I was busy in the kitchen. With the regular staff sent home because of the storm, it was down to me to make sure your meals weren't cold."

"You're a trained chef?"

Angus chuckled. "That I'm not. But we have an excellent cook who plated everything before leaving, so it just needed warming. The castle facilities are modern, so it was no chore."

"You were in the kitchen the entire time we ate and then stayed in there after you cleared the table?" I asked.

Angus hesitated for a second. "After the kitchen was set for the next course, I took a breather while the food warmed. Just a short one. I didn't leave until Juliet was happy with how things were progressing, though."

"How long was she with you?"

"A few minutes."

"Where did you go after you left the kitchen?" I asked.

"To my cottage. It's just off the rear garden, so close."

"How long did it take you to get there?"

"It's a three-minute walk if you keep your head down and get your heart pumping."

"You went out in this weather?"

Angus chuckled again. "I'm a Scotsman, Miss Vale. A bit of snow doesn't frighten me. And I've walked home in worse. I needed my tobacco tin."

"Do you live alone?"

He nodded. "Aye. Always have. There's been no one bonny enough to catch my eye."

I held back a smile. "Not even Ruby?"

His cheeks flushed. "Well, she is lovely."

"Yes, and impressionable, so have a care there," I cautioned.

Angus acknowledged my warning with a nod.

"What happened when you returned to the castle?" I asked.

"That's when I passed the Thistle Inn office window. The light was on, which made me curious. I didn't think anyone would be in there, given you were all dining. I glanced through the window, and at first, I thought Constance had fallen asleep at her desk."

"And when she didn't stir, that was when you sounded the alarm?"

"It took me a second to see the knife and the blood. After all, it's not what you'd expect. Then I came to my senses. I called for Gregor's help, since he was the closest, and then ran to the pub. I tried the door and found it locked. That was when I ran to the dining room to fetch help."

"You didn't think to get inside the office first and assist Constance?"

Angus rubbed the back of his neck, a flicker of something pained behind his eyes. "To be honest, panic had me by the throat. Nothing prepares you for coming across someone you know, lying like that. I thought..." He swallowed. "Well, I wasn't thinking clearly. Perhaps I should have broken down the door or smashed a window."

"Death never gets easier," I said. "No matter how many times you meet it."

His gaze flicked to me, surprised. "You speak from experience?"

"Let's just say I was busy during the war."

Angus didn't press further, although his gaze was full of curiosity.

"What happened next?" I asked.

"You know the rest," Angus said. "We all went to the office, you got inside, and that's when we discovered Constance was beyond help. Maybe... maybe I should have done more."

"You did what you could. No one would expect you to know how to handle something like this."

Angus gave a quiet grunt of agreement, but he didn't look convinced.

"Did you see any signs of how our killer fled the scene?" I asked.

"Nothing that seemed obvious to me. What should I have looked for?"

"Footsteps in the snow. Damp marks on the floor if the killer had snuck in from outside. Anything could be useful."

"I'm no help in that regard. I had my head down against the snow as I walked, focused on keeping upright. It was only the light that caught my eye. Then everything happened so quickly," Angus said. "I could have missed something."

I paused. "You said you'd forgotten about the servants' tunnels in the castle. That's a significant detail to forget."

"I wasn't thinking about the tunnels. I only remembered them when Gregor brought them up."

"Given that a tunnel leads directly to the Thistle Inn office, it could have been our killer's route in or out. That would leave no footprints in the snow."

"True enough, but we all searched the tunnels and found nothing."

"What does that lead you to believe?" I asked.

A silence fell between us.

"You think it was one of the family?" Angus's voice was soft.

"I think it's more likely to be someone Constance knew than a stranger," I said. "And although several of you spotted movement outside, no one confirmed who or what it was."

"Do you think someone made it up?"

"Perhaps to cover their guilt."

His shoulders sagged. "But who would do such an awful thing?"

"Did Constance mention anything to you in the days leading up to her murder? Anyone or anything that bothered her?"

"Not to me. But she wasn't the confiding type. We spoke mostly about furnishings for the wedding and access points for the guests. I helped where I could, since I'm aware Juliet can be... demanding. Nothing was ever good enough for her. That put a strain on Constance."

I smiled faintly. "Juliet has changed little since our Sunday school days. Did Constance ever seem overwhelmed?"

"Now and then. I saw her outside one evening, having a smoke behind the kitchen wing. She looked tired."

"Did you ask her about it?"

"No. I brought her a cup of tea but said nothing." He sighed. "That poor lass didn't deserve this end."

"Is there anything else you can think of to help us find Constance's killer?" I asked.

Angus leaned forward. "There was one thing. It could be nothing, but a week or so back, I saw Constance stuffing something into a large bag. She jumped when she saw me watching her, like I'd caught her thieving the silver."

"What was it?" I asked.

"I didn't get a look. I even made a joke about if any silverware went missing, I'd know who to speak to, and she snapped at me and told me to knock next time, even though the door was open, so I didn't have any reason to announce myself."

"What was Constance hiding?" I murmured more to myself than to Angus.

He shook his head. "I can't help you there. But that was the only time I ever saw her lose her composure."

"She must have come close, working for Juliet," I said.

Angus's confident smile returned. "I've seen some near misses. Dealing with high society clients must give you an iron will and the strength to bite your tongue many times a day."

"It must. Thank you. I have everything I need," I said. "Please ask Gregor to join me."

Angus squared his shoulders. "Is that necessary? He's not always confident around people, but I'll vouch for his character. He's a good man and has been here longer than anyone else."

"Then he'll have a wealth of information for me."

"That wasn't my meaning. Gregor never pokes his nose where it's not welcome." Angus stood and folded his arms. "He always kept clear of Constance. There was no conflict, so no reason for bad blood. Gregor has old-fashioned values and a strict moral code."

"I don't have the luxury of ruling anyone out," I said. "Gregor is a castle employee, and he had access to the Thistle Inn. That's enough to ensure I must question him. If for no other reason than to provide me with information to fill in my knowledge."

A pause hung between us, filled with the muffled groan of wind around the ancient windows.

Angus gave a curt nod. "I'll ask him to come in."

As the door clicked shut behind him, I leaned back in the chair, letting the fire warm my hands. Angus had held his own. He was calm and direct. He'd answered everything I asked without a single slip, but that didn't mean he was in the clear.

Angus had the opportunity, and he had no alibi, since no one could verify his whereabouts at the time of the murder. And he'd found the body. Was his panic a ruse?

I let out a soft sigh. But what of his motive? I'd yet to find one. Angus hadn't disliked Constance. If anything, he seemed quietly fond of her or at least respectful. Still, there was that mystery about what Constance had hidden from him. Had Angus seen what she'd concealed in a bag? And was it valuable enough to kill for?

"This won't do, Benji," I muttered. "Why won't the killer simply put his hand in the air and let the desire to clear his guilt win?"

Benji rested his head on my knee and looked up at me in a way that suggested he was in full agreement.

There were too many readily available suspects, and that never pleased me. One more to go. It was time to see what Gregor, the castle's oldest and most faithful watchman, might reveal.

Chapter 14

Gregor stood in the doorway, cap in hand, his posture straight despite the years carved into his frame. His coat was worn at the cuffs, and snow still clung to his boots in melting patches. He must have needed a breath of air to escape the tension, much like I did.

"Miss Vale," he said with a respectful dip of the head.

"Thank you for coming to see me, Gregor. Please come in and take a seat. The fire's warm."

He hesitated before lowering himself into the chair opposite me, his eyes flicking around the room like he was memorising every detail.

I recognised his caution. It wasn't fear, just a deep-set wariness that came from decades of keeping one's head down in a house full of privilege.

Benji stirred from his spot by the fire and trotted over, his tail giving a gentle thump against the carpet. He nudged Gregor's knee with his nose.

"Well now, are you in need of a scratch behind the ears?" Gregor's face softened instantly. "That's a fine lad you've got there."

"Indeed, he is. And Benji's an excellent judge of character," I said. "He likes you already."

Gregor offered a hand, and Benji leaned into it.

"I had a dog like this when I was a boy." Gregor's voice warmed. "Not as pretty in the coat, but loyal. His name was Fergus. My father gave him to me when I turned ten. That dog followed me through every hallway and hedge until the day he passed."

"He sounds like an outstanding companion," I said.

Gregor gave a small nod. "Better than some people, if you don't mind me saying."

"I don't mind at all. I usually enjoy the company of dogs more than I do people."

He let out a short laugh. "That's a good notion to have."

"I volunteer at a home for unwanted dogs in London. I've made some of my happiest memories there."

"That sounds like a fine way to spend time." Gregor kept stroking Benji.

"Perhaps you could get a dog here," I said. "Another companion."

"I would, but the family don't approve." He sighed. "It's a pity. They always chase off trouble."

"Trouble like we find ourselves in." I waited a beat before adding, "I know this situation is unsettling, but you've worked here longer than anyone, so I'm hoping you can help me understand the lay of the land."

"I'll do what I can," Gregor said.

"While we all sat down for dinner, where did you go?"

"I left the castle just after seven, Miss," he replied. "I went back to my quarters, which are above the old stables."

"Do you live alone?"

"Aye, I do." He looked a touch sheepish. "My work keeps me busy."

"Living on your own is nothing to be ashamed of. If my mother didn't place so many demands on my time, I'd have a little place of my own. Just Benji and me."

Gregor's brow furrowed. "Didn't I hear you had a fellow?"

I tilted my head. "You are observant."

His cheeks flushed. "I'm sorry. I didn't mean to overhear something private."

"That's quite all right. And your observational skills could serve me," I said. "And yes, to answer your question, I have a wonderful chap, but we're both independent. If we lived together, one of us would perish. And not from natural causes."

Gregor laughed again. "Living alone has its benefits. And the family looks after me. I've been in the area since I was fifteen, and my father worked here before me. He taught me everything I know."

"I'm pleased to hear you're supported," I said. "Returning to Constance's death, did you see anyone doing anything out of character this evening that made you worried?"

He shook his head slowly. "No one. But I was outdoors or in the barns most of the time. The weather was just as bad as it is now, so I'd have been surprised to see anyone outside."

"Which means no one saw you either."

Gregor hesitated. "That's true. But the storm was blowing, and I kept my head down, so maybe I was seen. Does it matter?"

I didn't answer his question. "When did you find out about Constance?"

"When Angus hammered on my door," Gregor said. "He was like a banshee at the bell. I thought the castle roof had come off by the way he was shouting. He told me there'd been trouble and the wedding lady was injured. I thought he meant Miss Juliet at first."

"Did you know Constance well?"

Gregor scratched his jaw. "Hardly at all. She wasn't one for lingering and was always marching from one room to another. Most likely in a hurry to keep up with all the work given to her."

I watched Gregor carefully. He hadn't looked me in the eye since he'd sat down, but there was no guile in him, just the mild discomfort of a man unused to being questioned by a woman.

"You did sterling work getting us into the locked office," I said.

Gregor shifted. "It were no use though. She was gone."

"Did you see anything out of place in the office?"

He frowned, searching his memory. "I've never been in there. I enjoy a few pints at the bar, but the office isn't a place I go. There's no reason for me to be there. And I prefer to be outside. Even in weather like this."

"Was there ever any ill feeling between you and Constance?"

His head came up fast. "Me? No, Miss. I didn't hardly speak to her. We had no quarrel."

"But did she ever speak sharply to you? Ask for something unreasonable for the wedding?"

Gregor scratched the back of his neck. "She once asked me to fetch supplies from the cellar for a wine tasting. It wasn't my job, but I didn't want to offend her."

"Did that annoy you?"

"The task wasn't the issue, but she forgot she'd sent me and had the door locked while I was still in there." A brief smile ghosted across his face. "I was down there near an hour before she realised. She apologised after and said Sir Frederick had taken her focus on another matter."

"Did she say what matter?"

"No, and it wasn't my place to ask," he said. "She brought me a biscuit and a cup of coffee to say sorry. I thought that was good of her."

"Yes, it was. And not quite a motive for murder," I murmured.

"No, Miss! I'd never harm a lass." Gregor hesitated. "She always looked burdened. Like she was carrying more than wedding plans. I don't know what it was, but I'd see her sometimes, standing in a corridor, staring like she'd lost something."

"But you never asked her if anything was amiss?"

"I know when to hold my tongue." Gregor drew in a breath, opened his mouth, but then stopped.

"Is there something else? I asked.

"I... I don't wish to speak unkindly about any member of this family, but Lord Robert concerns me. Did you notice how he watched Constance?"

"He's certainly observant of women's figures." My tone was caustic. "My manners insist I say something along the lines of: Lord Robert is a traditional gentleman who believes women are only here for the amusement and entertainment of men."

"That sounds about right. There's not much difference in our ages," Gregor said, "but I value a woman for more than her ... well, her looks."

"Women across the world rejoice in that fact," I said.

That drew a small smile from Gregor's lips. "I saw nothing more than the way he watched Constance, but it made me uncomfortable, and it must have done her. She never stayed long in his company."

"Did Constance say anything to you about her concerns?"

"No! But I can't stay quiet. What happened to that young lady is wrong. I have a niece her age, and it chills my blood to think of anything happening to her because a man thinks he has a right to do improper things."

"You're an excellent fellow, Gregor," I said. "And I appreciate your honesty. It took great courage to tell me."

"I know revealing my worries about Lord Robert could land me in trouble, but I must do so." Gregor gave a small, stiff nod, the kind a man gives when he's trying to keep his dignity while his heart rattles against his ribs.

"One more thing. Did you ever observe Constance in conversation with Juliet or Sir Frederick? Anything that gave you pause?"

He rubbed his palms against his knees. "Juliet's got a temper when she's pushed, but Constance knew how to sidestep it. I'd say they respected each other. Well, as far as that goes, when one lady is issuing the orders and the other's meant to say yes to everything."

"Did they ever argue? Even quietly?"

"I saw a moment near the dining room. Juliet was red in the face, and Constance had her arms folded. I was far off, so I didn't hear the words, but Juliet stamped away. Constance just stood there and looked at her notepad."

"Did you think it was serious?"

"I couldn't say. But Constance wasn't the type to stand firm unless she had reason."

"And what about Sir Frederick?"

Gregor hesitated again.

"You've already been more help than you know, but if there's something else, now is the time to reveal it."

He looked pained. "I wouldn't say Sir Frederick was unkind, but he'd been tense these past days. Constance was working harder than ever, and it seemed every time I passed her, she had a new list or change to manage."

"Did she say anything about him being unreasonable?"

"No, Miss! Not a word. But Constance watched him out of the corner of her eye."

"Why do you think that was?" I asked.

Gregor exhaled through his nose. "It's just a feeling, mind you, but I wondered if he'd said something. Something she wouldn't have welcomed. Miss Constance always kept things professional."

"Are you suggesting Sir Frederick had feelings for her?"

"I wouldn't presume. But he looked at her differently than he did the other staff. Though that might have just been the wedding weighing on him."

It was subtle but troubling information.

"Thank you," I said at last. "That's all for now. You've given me plenty to think about."

"If I can help more, just say the word." Gregor patted Benji again then left. When he was gone, I reached down and scratched behind Benji's ears.

"Well, boy," I murmured, "Gregor was a helpful observer, but one also lacking an alibi. However, where is his motive? Being accidentally locked in a wine cellar wouldn't prompt unhinged rage."

Benji wagged his tail.

"And you like Gregor, so I'm putting him at the bottom of the list," I said. "But someone is hiding the truth and keeping things from us. The question is, which secret was worth killing for?"

Chapter 15

The scent of toast and strong tea was enough to lure the dead from their slumber. Or at least, it roused me after my late night to bed after questioning the suspects.

"I hope you're awake," Ruby whispered, nudging the bedroom door closed with her slippered foot. "I risked life and limb in the kitchen for this. Although I'm delighted to report nothing got burned!"

Benji lifted his head from the foot of the bed, his tail wagging, as she tiptoed across the thick rug with a full tray in hand.

"You're an angel." I sat up and accepted the steaming mug she passed me. "And you did far better than I would have done."

"I know. You're a horror in the kitchen." Ruby climbed in beside me, her hair still pinned. "I couldn't sleep, and I thought you might be the same, what with all those motives, alibis, and opportunities rattling around in your head."

"My dreams were vivid," I said. "Where's Grace?"

"Happily sleeping. That child is the real angel. She definitely read the how to be a perfect baby book twice." Ruby offered me a slice of toast, thickly buttered, but broke the corner off for Benji, who crunched it like a gentleman.

Outside, the snowstorm had eased, and from the glimpse I saw from the window, the castle lay blanketed in thick white silence.

Ruby licked a smear of butter from her thumb. "Last night was eventful."

"To say the least." I wrapped my hands around my teacup and let the heat sink into my fingers.

"And? We barely had a chance to talk because we were fixing the office door with Angus and Gregor and appropriately covering Constance."

"I'm glad we took the time to do that. It felt disrespectful to leave her exposed." It had taken an hour to locate coverings and secure a piece of wood to cover the hole made in the office door.

"It was the right thing to do." Ruby fed Benji more crust. "So..."

"I have suspects, motives, alibis, some flimsy, and most likely a few lies. But no idea who killed Constance."

"Let's go over it all. Talk me through them."

I sipped my tea. "Juliet left the table just before Constance was killed to check on Angus. But there were no witnesses during the time she was away from the kitchen. Angus said she left him after a few minutes, so that would have given her time."

"And her motive?"

"Constance threatened to walk away from the wedding," I said. "That would have ruined everything."

Ruby nodded. "Juliet would cope poorly with the scandal if her highly anticipated wedding went wrong. Who's next?"

"Before we move on, Gregor mentioned Freddie behaved oddly around Constance. I wondered if he'd made overtures to Constance and Juliet found out."

"Goodness! And Juliet killed her in a jealous rage?"

"Possibly. Freddie insisted it wasn't someone from the wedding party, though."

"Well, that's only natural. He'd never implicate his betrothed," Ruby said. "Is he hiding what he tried to do with Constance?"

"He could have admired her more than he should have."

Ruby hummed. "But he was at the table with you, so he didn't stick the knife in."

"I suggested he had someone else do it."

"And his response?"

"Outrage!"

"No surprise there. Has he the backbone for such devious tactics?"

"Probably not, but I wanted to see how he behaved under pressure."

"Good for you. Go on. Next suspect," Ruby said.

"Lord Robert is arrogant and foul."

"I heartily agree. Let's pick him as our killer and be done with it."

"If only it were that simple." I smiled. "He claims not to have known Constance, but he watched her more closely than he admits. Gregor said Constance avoided his company."

"As do I. He's a repulsive old chap. Every time he looks at me, I get shivers, and not the kind that make me giddy and excited. But we have the same issue with Lord Robert. You are his alibi."

"Which is unfortunate. I also put it to him that he arranged for someone to murder Constance."

Ruby chortled. "And I can imagine how well that was received."

"He was also outraged! His pomposity had his veins bulging. Perhaps I should have been kinder because of his age, but the man riles me."

"I'm glad you gave his cage a good rattle and put him in his place."

"Sadly, a chap with old money and entitlement knows exactly where his place is."

Ruby bared her teeth. "It's most unfair. What about Lady Sophia?"

"She was dismissive of the wedding and of me. She hinted at an inappropriate closeness between Constance and Frederick, too."

"Didn't she leave the table?"

"Yes, and she has no alibi, claiming to have returned to her room. But she could have slipped away to the office when no one watched."

"There's something devious about Lady Sophia," Ruby said. "It wouldn't surprise me if she were involved. What about our charming Scotsman? Please tell me I have nothing to fear from him."

"Angus had an opportunity," I continued. "He was managing dinner alone. And all he had to do was warm the food and serve it, so he would have had time to get to the Thistle Inn."

Ruby pouted. "What about his motive?"

"There's no obvious motive, although he mentioned seeing Constance concealing something in a bag not so long ago. I wondered if he saw what it was and coveted it."

"That's rather vague." Ruby finished her toast. "I'm convinced he's innocent."

"Because you want to see more of him in that kilt."

"Why not? He's terribly dashing. What about Gregor?"

"It's the same tale with Gregor," I said. "He was in his quarters above the stables and swears he barely spoke to Constance during her time here. He was helpful, though, and provided me with plenty to mull over."

Ruby was quiet for a moment. "The poor girl. How unfair that this happened to her, and the killer hopes to escape without consequence."

Benji let out a soft sigh, resting his chin on Ruby's knee, his hopeful gaze on the remaining pieces of toast.

"We won't let that happen," I said.

"So?" Ruby asked after she'd eaten a second slice of toast and fed more crust to Benji. "What's your gut telling you?"

I glanced out at the grey light pressing against the frosted windowpane. "That the killer is waiting to see what we'll do next."

"I propose we quiz the lot of them over porridge and kippers," Ruby said.

I tilted my head thoughtfully. "Or we listen and watch. People say the most revealing things when they think no one is listening. That's how Gregor learned so much about the family."

"We need to split up," Ruby said. "Casual conversation, small groups. If we corner the same suspect together, they'll panic and refuse to say anything, so we'll make no progress."

"Agreed. I want to focus on Juliet, so you watch Lady Sophia. Maybe get her on the topic of weddings again. That lit a fire under her last night. I only had to say the word divorce, and her hackles lifted like a wildcat."

"She'll combust if I prod at her. What fun!" Ruby said, grinning. "One divorce and she's over love. Isn't that a tragedy?"

"Whereas you are a hopeless romantic. I'm unsure which one is worse."

"No, Veronica," she said in all seriousness. "I'm a hopeful romantic. Wherever there is hope, there is a glimmer of the possible."

"Very well. Hopeful." I gently squeezed Ruby's hand, glad the traumas she'd experienced hadn't swerved her off course for too long. "And where have you focused your romantic hope this time? Or can I guess at a certain handsome, kilt wearing chap with a friendly wink?"

Before Ruby could reply, a knock rattled the door. It was firm, hurried, followed by a muffled, "Miss Vale? Are you decent?"

Benji gave a low woof, his ears up, but his reaction suggested we shouldn't be alarmed.

I slid out of bed and cracked the door open to find Angus in the corridor, his cheeks flushed. "Is something the matter?"

"My apologies for disturbing you. But you'd best come quick. There's been a break-in."

I blinked. "Where?"

"The Thistle Inn office," he said grimly. "Someone's been inside during the night. I found the wood taken down."

Ruby was already out of bed, her expression tight as she listened.

"Give us two minutes and we'll join you." I slid the door shut, grabbed the nearest clothing and boots, and ushered Ruby out to do the same.

Once dressed, we followed Angus down the stairs and into the main hallway, my mind racing as we dashed through the bar of the Thistle Inn, the air chilled due to the lack of fire.

If someone had come back during the night, it meant they'd been looking for something. Or worse, trying to hide an incriminating clue they thought they'd left behind. A clue I'd missed.

The heavy oak door to the office was ajar, and the panel placed across the opening removed.

"Touch nothing, but inspect everything," I said as we crossed the threshold.

Ruby nudged the door fully open with her shoulder, and Benji padded in beside us, his nose twitching.

The desk was as we'd left it, and Constance's body was still covered. I turned to the shelves, the drawers, and the paper stacks, taking it all in.

"I heard no sounds of someone breaking in last night," Ruby said.

"Your rooms are so far from the inn entrance, they'd have needed to make a hell of a racket to get you to stir," Angus said.

"From what I can recall, nothing looks different." Ruby crouched beside the desk.

"If someone was after something, they knew where to find it without making a mess," I said.

The place didn't look like it had been turned over. I moved to the cabinet near the far wall. A drawer was open an inch or two. I slipped my fingers into the gap and peeked in. The files were in place. A couple of envelopes were slightly off-angle, but nothing that screamed tampering.

Angus frowned. "Or they could have been looking for something specific, but they were disturbed before they got their hands on it."

"Do you and Gregor check the castle at night?" I asked.

"No. Once the doors are locked, that's it for the night."

Benji gave a low whine near Constance's still form. He sniffed the air then looked at me with questioning eyes.

I crouched beside him, my fingers brushing his warm fur. "It doesn't feel right, does it?"

Ruby glanced over, and her gaze flicked to Constance. "Should we... I mean, check her?"

Angus shifted his weight, his face tight with uncertainty. "It feels wrong, disturbing her like that. But if someone came in here, and they took something from her..."

"Then we need to be sure." I looked at Constance's shrouded form.

We stood around her in silence for a moment, as though asking her permission. Then I nodded. "Let's make it quick and careful."

Angus moved to one side of the body, Ruby to the other. I gently lifted the edge of the fabric. Constance lay as we had left her, her profile peaceful, betraying nothing of the violence done to her. The knife was still there, lodged between her shoulder blades.

"Don't touch her, but we'll check her pockets," I whispered.

Ruby and I set to work, being careful not to move anything. After a minute, I sat back on my heels. Nothing was out of place.

"If anyone took an item from Constance's body, they were jolly tidy about it." I gently placed the cover back over Constance. "I didn't anticipate this would happen. We'll have to ensure it doesn't occur again. We'll post someone at the door tonight."

"A rota," Ruby said brightly. "We can take turns. I'll do the first shift. I'll bring Grace with me. Her crying will keep anyone away."

Angus smiled. "I haven't heard that wee angel cry once since you've arrived."

"You can thank the thick walls for that." Ruby's smile softened. "But she is such a good baby."

Before we could progress the rota idea, footsteps echoed on the polished floor behind us, and Lady Sophia appeared in the doorway like a stage actress making her grand entrance.

"There you all are!" She lifted a perfectly shaped brow. "You do know breakfast has been served, yes? Or has murder replaced marmalade as our morning ritual?"

Ruby straightened slowly. "We've been busy. Someone broke into the office overnight."

Lady Sophia swept her gaze across the room, took in the body beneath the cover, and gave an exaggerated sigh. "Yes, well, if we must talk blood and bodies, can we at least be civilised and do it over coffee? And preferably before the toast gets cold. Although Juliet made it, so goodness knows what it will be like."

"You're not curious about who broke in?" Angus asked.

"Why bother? I already assume everyone here is lying about something. I find it saves time." With that, she pivoted and swept back down the hall.

"Lady Sophia is a menace," Ruby muttered.

"She also has a point." I gently ushered everyone out of the office, and Angus settled the panel of wood against the opening. "It's time to revisit our suspects and see what someone got up to overnight."

The dining room table had been messily set with china and gleaming cutlery. There was a jug of coffee, and toast racks stood between pots of orange marmalade and raspberry jam.

Juliet was placing the last rack of toast down with a flourish and a smile when we entered. "Look at me. I'm already the perfect housewife. Freddie is thrilled."

"There are maids who'll do that for you, if you have any sense." Lady Sophia settled into a chair and inspected the butter with visible suspicion.

I took a seat opposite Lord Robert, and Ruby sat next to me, Benji between us.

"If no one objects, I'd like Gregor to join us," Angus said.

"He's the hired help!" Lady Sophia protested.

"The man deserves to be kept informed," Ruby said.

"Let Angus inform him while Gregor mucks out the stables," Lady Sophia said.

"There are no horses to muck out," Angus said levelly.

"I'm happy for him to be here," Juliet said. "Freddie?"

"Oh, of course. This situation is unique, so I see no harm." Freddie looked up from his plate.

Angus nodded and dashed out.

While we waited for him to return with Gregor, Ruby attended to coffee, while I fixed us more toast.

Angus appeared, a bashful Gregor in tow. Angus took a seat, but Gregor remained standing by the wall, unsure whether he was meant to join us.

"Please," I said gently, gesturing to an empty chair. "You're part of this household, Gregor."

He murmured a quiet thanks and sat, folding his large hands in his lap, not touching anything in front of him.

I let my gaze move slowly around the table. "Before we eat, or enjoy anything resembling normality, I must ask for your attention. We discovered this morning that someone returned to the office in the Thistle Inn during the night. Nothing appears to have been taken, but I must ask why someone in this castle would go back to the scene of the crime."

Juliet paled. Freddie's coffee cup paused halfway to his lips.

"What are you accusing us of?" Lady Sophia asked.

"No one is accusing anyone," I said, "but I'd like to know what each of you did last night after retiring."

Lady Sophia rolled her eyes. "Is this a breakfast or an inquisition?"

"Both, I'm afraid. You saw the scene in the Thistle Inn."

"Splendid," she muttered. "Pass the jam. If I'm to be interrogated, I refuse to do it on an empty stomach."

"We'll begin simply," I said. "Did anyone leave their room after retiring?"

There was a beat of silence.

Freddie cleared his throat. "I thought I heard a noise. Some sort of scratching outside. I assumed it was a shutter, or the storm had knocked something loose."

"You didn't investigate?" I asked.

"No," he said. "I... truthfully, I didn't want to find anything. Everything that happened to Constance unsettled me. I peeked out the window and looked in the corridor but then closed my door and put a chair against it."

"I don't see the point of this," Lady Sophia said. "No one will admit to wandering about in the dark after a murder. We'll all say we were in bed. The killer most likely of all."

I ignored her. "Lord Robert, let's continue with you."

He gave a gravelly, prolonged sigh as though I'd just asked him to surrender his entire fortune. "I was asleep in the green room. Heavily asleep, I'll have you know. These infernal pills make a man unconscious for hours."

"And you woke when?"

"When Angus bellowed along the corridor like a dying moose this morning," he said. "Do ask him to keep it down the next time he needs to so vigorously exercise his lungs."

Angus barely hid his scowl. "My apologies, Lord Robert. The break in surprised me, and I wanted Veronica to know as soon as possible because I knew it was important to her investigation."

Lady Sophia snorted into her cup.

I turned to Juliet. "And you?"

"I went to bed shortly after you interviewed me," she said. "I didn't sleep well, though. There was too much on my mind."

I nodded. "Did you hear anything?"

"A bang. Maybe something falling, but like Freddie, I thought it was the dratted storm."

"Gregor?" I asked. "Did you see or hear anything?"

Gregor looked as though he wished the floor would open and swallow him. "I sleep above the old stables, so castle noise isn't something I can help with."

"What about seeing anyone outside?"

"Are we back to the deranged killer skulking in the snowstorm theory? How very dull," Lady Sophia said.

Gregor gulped. "I didn't stir all night. I saw and heard nothing."

"And you, Angus?" I asked.

"You already know I'm housed away from the castle," he said. "And I don't come back until the morning, so I'm no help to you."

"Thank you," I said. "Now, here's what concerns me. Someone broke into the office, but did no damage. If they'd secured the panel over the broken door after they'd been inside, Angus wouldn't have spotted anything amiss. Which means they knew exactly what they were looking for."

No one spoke.

Benji gave a soft growl, and Ruby absently passed him a bit of toast under the table.

"Someone risked exposure," I said. "So, the prize they sought must have been worth the risk. If any of you remembers anything about last night, this is the time to speak."

Still silence.

Lady Sophia daintily buttered her toast. "Since that little drama achieved nothing, may I suggest we enjoy what remains of breakfast before we're accused of setting the place alight, too?"

My appetite diminished, and my anger rose. "I need fresh air."

Benji jumped up, his tail wagging.

Ruby grimaced as her gaze flicked to the frosty window. "Shall I come with you?"

"Finish your breakfast. I need to think." I left the table, my thoughts muddled. Someone in this room had lied to me, but I couldn't find a clue as to who it was.

As I surveyed everyone, Gregor caught my eye, holding my gaze for several seconds before standing, too.

"I should get to work," he said.

"There's nothing much to do while the weather is so bad," Angus said. "Stay and have something to eat. There's plenty of food."

"I've always got something to keep me busy. I'll check the woodpile." Gregor glanced at me again before scurrying out.

I collected Benji and followed, nearly bumping into Gregor as I rounded the corner. He'd been waiting for me.

"Excuse me," I began.

"I'm sorry to bother you, Miss Vale," he said. "I didn't know how to approach you in front of the others without drawing attention."

"Is there something bothering you?" I asked.

Gregor pressed his lips together. "I asked Angus about you last night after you questioned everyone."

"Is there anything in particular you'd like to know about me?"

"You deal with the dead, don't you?"

"In a manner of speaking. I write their obituaries," I said.

His tongue darted across his lower lip. "Do you come across many murders?"

"Some. Most people pass from natural causes, but there are always tragic cases. I ensure people remember those individuals for the right reasons, not for the injustices they endured."

"Much like Constance," Gregor said, his expression darkening.

"Why the interest in my experience with those who have been murdered? Is there something you need to tell me about Constance?" I asked.

Before he could answer, footsteps approached, and Angus rounded the corner. "Oh! Hello there. Is Gregor helping you with something?"

"He is indeed!" I expanded no further, looking expectantly at Angus, trying to hide my irritation at being disturbed.

"Well, whatever it is, it will have to wait." Angus drew in a breath. "I know where the killer got the murder weapon!"

Chapter 16

"How did you figure that out?" I asked Angus, stepping towards him, my attention taken from Gregor and whatever he'd been about to reveal.

"I knew something was amiss when we were in the Thistle Inn office, but I couldn't put my finger on it," Angus said. "I kept turning it over in my head, and the answer suddenly hit me."

"Then let's not waste time." I gestured for him to move.

"Gregor, gather the others," Angus said. "We'll find what we're looking for in the Thistle Inn."

I hesitated. Was revealing this new piece of the puzzle to all a wise endeavour? Before I could stop Gregor, he was off like a whippet, and Angus wasn't much slower, so I hastened to catch up with them, Benji by my side.

All heads turned as we entered the dining room.

"We're reconvening in the Thistle Inn," I said without preamble. "There's been a development in the case."

Lady Sophia rolled her eyes. "Must we parade after you like obedient hounds? If the killer wishes to strike again, I vote we let him. It would liven things up."

"Let's hope he starts with you," Ruby muttered as she joined me by the door.

Benji growled softly in agreement.

"It's important," Angus said. "I discovered how the killer got their hands on such a wicked blade. I knew I recognised the handle, but the shock of the situation left me drawing a blank until just now."

Lady Sophia tossed aside her napkin. "I'm practically breathless with excitement."

We moved in a slow procession through the castle. Fresh snow gusted outside the windows as another heavy, grey cloud darkened the morning. Gregor trailed at the back of the group, his steps slow. Angus walked ahead, grim and focused, like a man leading a funeral procession.

Once we were inside the Thistle Inn, we waited for Angus to remove the wood panel. He peered inside and nodded as if convincing himself he'd been right.

"Angus, the floor is yours," I said.

He nodded, tugged slightly at his collar, then turned to face the group. "It was only when I was thinking over the break-in that it struck me. The knife used to kill Constance was in here this entire time. Or rather, a Scottish dagger known as a dirk. And it has a twin." He pointed at a display cabinet to the left of the desk.

"I see no knives," Lady Sophia said.

I walked over and crouched beside the cabinet. I had to peer over several other objects before eyeing a velvet cradle where the dirk should have been. The twin blade still nestled in place, its carved handle glinting beneath the glass.

"It looks more decorative than an actual weapon," I murmured. "Are they identical?"

Angus nodded. "The same make, and the same inlaid grip. Decorative, not practical."

"And yet one was used to stab Constance in the back," I said.

"It makes no sense," Freddie said from behind me. "Why use something so ornate and traceable? And there are sharper knives in the kitchen that would have done a better job."

"A better job than killing a woman?" Lady Sophia gave a gentle snort of disbelief. "Were they planning on gutting her, too, but the dirk wasn't sharp enough?"

"That's quite enough of that." Juliet pressed a hand to her cheek, and her eyes fluttered.

Angus folded his arms. "Perhaps someone wanted to use that dirk for a specific reason. But here's the part you need to hear. A few weeks ago, I came in here and found Tommy with the cabinet open."

"My landlord?" I asked. "Why would he need a dirk?"

"He said he'd been asked to sharpen them for a display at the wedding." Angus met my gaze. "When I asked who'd made the request, he said a family member. At the time, I didn't think to ask who. But now... well, perhaps I should."

"Did he seem uneasy being given that task?" Ruby asked.

Angus shook his head. "Not especially. He just muttered something about keeping up appearances for the guests. It seemed as if he thought it was a normal request."

Juliet stepped forward, her brow creased. "I didn't ask for the dirks to be cleaned, sharpened, or displayed for my wedding. I didn't even know they were here. We have so many pieces like that. They're usually gifts and end up hidden in a cabinet because we don't know what else to do with them."

Lord Robert gave a derisive splutter. "They're display pieces. All this fuss over a pair of oversized toothpicks. It proves nothing."

"You didn't ask for them to be sharpened?" I turned to him.

"Certainly not," he said.

I focused back on Angus. "The killer must have planned to use this blade and had to ensure it was sharp enough to do the job."

"And Tommy knew the killer well enough not to question the order," Ruby said, her gaze on the Augustine family members.

My gaze flicked to them, too, not excluding Freddie. Any of them could have accessed the Thistle Inn and issued the request without raising eyebrows.

"Is the use of a dirk significant?" I asked. "Do these blades hold a meaning?"

"It could be important," Angus replied. "As Sir Frederick said, there are better and sharper blades in the castle. People use dirks for thrusting or stabbing, but these handles are carved and inlaid with gems. It would have been uncomfortable to hold."

"Perhaps the killer panicked," Juliet suggested. "They didn't expect Constance to appear, so they grabbed the closest weapon and hid, waiting for her to settle at the desk before attacking."

"But why did someone in this family ask for the dirks to be sharpened?" I queried. "That suggests premeditation. And the cabinet door where the dirks were stored was closed when I entered the room on the night of the murder. If the killer had time to select a weapon and close the door, they had time to pick a better blade."

"Who gifted them to the family?" Ruby asked.

Juliet pursed her lips. "Possibly King George. Sophia, do you recall?"

"I haven't the foggiest," she replied. "If the jewels were something I could wear, then I'd have been interested in them."

"Did Constance slight the Scottish family heritage, and someone decided she needed punishing? The dirk was a statement," I said.

"I can't imagine it was that. She spoke respectfully about everybody," Juliet said. "And she was thrilled to visit Scotland for work. Constance told me how much she enjoyed the wild landscape."

"She'd have told you anything to ensure she received her wage." Lady Sophia appeared bored as she moved to the back of the small group.

I took a final look around. Had the killer come back last night because of the dirks? Removing them would have muddied the situation, but they were both here. It was possible they'd been disturbed before taking the other dirk.

"Let's leave things as they are," I said. "Has anybody checked the telephone line this morning?"

"Countless times," Juliet said. "There's still not a peep out of it."

"Although the snow isn't so fierce, clearing the roads will take time, so it could be days before anyone makes the repairs to the line," Angus said.

"Don't say that," Juliet said. "I shudder to think of what will happen to Constance's body if she's left for so long."

"This room is chilly," I said. "There'll be little decay."

"How can you talk about such gruesome things?" Juliet asked.

"Death doesn't have to be gruesome," I said. "One must keep a practical head on one's shoulders when dealing with such a situation."

"How many dead bodies have you dealt with?" Freddie asked, a look of unmasked astonishment on his face.

"More than I care to mention." I gestured to the door, and the group swiftly made their way out of the Thistle Inn, talking among themselves.

I hung back, catching Ruby's arm and calling softly to Gregor to wait with us.

"What's going on?" Ruby whispered.

"Gregor was about to reveal something when Angus approached with his dirk revelation," I said.

Gregor glanced anxiously at Ruby.

"You may speak freely. I trust Ruby with my life," I said. "There are no secrets between us."

"Not anymore," Ruby murmured, glancing up at the nursery.

"Finish what you were about to tell me," I said to Gregor.

He drew in a breath. "I don't know if this is important."

"Does this have to do with the dirks?" Ruby asked.

Gregor shook his head, and a wave of indecision marred his forehead. "I don't want to get anyone in trouble."

"We want the killer in plenty of trouble," I said. "Have you remembered something?"

"No... I remembered it last night, but I wasn't sure I should say anything."

"But now it could be relevant?" I asked.

Gregor swallowed. "I saw Angus kiss Constance. It happened so fast that I couldn't believe my eyes."

"Gosh!" Ruby said.

"When did this happen?" I asked.

"About two weeks ago, just after supper had been served. I'd stayed on to lock up the back doors. They were alone in the corridor by the garden windows." He shifted his weight. "I didn't mean to linger, but I caught the moment clear as daylight."

"How did Constance respond?" I asked.

"She stepped back and smacked him across the chops!"

"My goodness! Constance didn't welcome the attention?" I asked.

"She marched away and left Angus holding his cheek."

Ruby's eyes were wide with surprise. "Did you ask Angus about it?"

"It's not my place. I debated even saying anything to you, but I wondered, what with everything going on, if it meant something."

"It could very well," I said. "Is Angus a man to give up on something he desires?"

"He has a stubborn streak, but I wouldn't call him bull-headed," Gregor said. "After that happened, he was cold towards Constance, and he stopped being so helpful."

Ruby let out a snort of disapproval. "Angus carried a grudge because Constance rejected him."

"She humiliated him," Gregor said, a note of defiance in his words, as if he felt he should support Angus.

"That behaviour is still inappropriate," I said. "You could be on to something, though. Angus has been jolly helpful."

Ruby leaned in. "Too helpful, do you think? Remembering information about the murder weapon was awfully convenient."

I nodded. "Perhaps Angus wants to make sure we look anywhere but at him."

Gregor gave a low grunt. "I thought the same thing, too. I respect the man, but I couldn't stop thinking about what happened to Constance."

"Do you think he's our killer?" Ruby sounded breathless.

"I think," I said, "Angus didn't mention that kiss when I questioned him about his opinion of Constance."

We let the silence stretch, the weight of it like frost in the air, as we mulled over that unpleasant reality.

"Thank you, Gregor," I said at last. "You were brave to reveal this information."

"Nothing to do with being brave. It was the right thing to do." He gave a respectful nod and disappeared down the corridor.

Ruby looked at me. "Where does this information leave us?"

I stared along the empty hall. "It leaves us with a man who had access, opportunity, and now, a motive."

Chapter 17

We found a quiet corner in the reading room just off the east corridor, far enough from the others to speak freely. Ruby sat on the edge of a leather armchair, while Benji settled between us, his chin resting on my foot.

"I still don't want it to be Angus," Ruby said. "And I know you'll tease me about the kilt, which I noticed he's not wearing today, but he's competent. Unflappable. The sort you trust to keep a place like this running, not panic and stab a woman in the back."

"That's exactly what makes him dangerous, if he is guilty," I said. "Angus knows every passage. Every weak spot. Every locked door and where to find the key. He'd have known about those dirks as well."

Ruby frowned. "Do you think it was just the slap from Constance? Maybe something else happened."

"I wondered about that," I said. "Angus has only worked here for two years, but that is enough time to establish himself."

"What are you thinking? He was pursuing other women?"

"Angus is a flirt but always keeps things respectful. At least, he does with us," I said. "He could be a different beast with other members of staff, especially the ones he oversees."

"Men with a little power can be dangerous creatures." Ruby wrinkled her nose.

"And what if Constance realised she wasn't the only one he'd made uncomfortable?" I suggested. "There are seasonal staff, kitchen girls, the scullery maids, and I even employ more help at the inn during the summer."

Ruby frowned. "Could a girl have confided in Constance?"

"If anyone was being harassed or treated improperly, it could have landed in her lap, even unofficially. If Constance was quietly gathering statements..."

"And Angus got wind of it," Ruby finished. "That would be far more dangerous."

"Ruination," I said. "He's well-respected here and told me with pride that this position was the making of him. If Constance accused him of impropriety and had others supporting her, he could be dismissed without a reference."

Ruby leaned back. "Angus doesn't strike me as a man who struggles for female attention, though. Why press himself on someone who isn't interested?"

"As you said, a little power makes people do foolish things."

We sat in silence for a moment, Benji pressing his head gently to my leg, sensing the tension in both of us.

Ruby straightened. "Whatever Constance had on him, she became a threat."

"And threats need to be snuffed out," I said. "Let's see what the ladies of the castle have to say about our loyal Angus."

"Do you think he tried to do something inappropriate to them?"

"He wouldn't have a job if he had, but perhaps a servant asked one of them for help."

"I pity any girl who asks Lady Sophia for assistance." Ruby stood. "Very well. Let's see what we can uncover."

A few moments later, we discovered Juliet and Lady Sophia in the blue parlour, the former reclining on a chaise with a velvet throw around her shoulders, while the latter was propped up by the window, sipping something far too strong for the early hour.

"He's being distant," Juliet said as we entered. "You don't think Freddie's gone off me, do you?"

"I think he's wondering why he agreed to marry into this family," Lady Sophia said.

Juliet turned tearful eyes on us. "Oh, Veronica, you'll tell me if Freddie says anything unkind, won't you?"

I blinked, surprised by the wobble in her voice. She looked genuinely stricken, as though a careless word might undo her entirely.

I hurried closer. "Juliet, are you quite well?"

She gave a tremulous smile, but it didn't reach her eyes. "Of course. It's just that Freddie has been distant. Not himself."

"Murder will do that to a chap." Lady Sophia turned her gaze to the window, although I didn't miss her smirk.

"It's been a dreadful couple of days," I said gently. "People are afraid and suspicious of each other. That would put anyone on edge."

"But what if he's changed his mind about me?" Juliet whispered. "What if all this chaos has made him see things differently? Maybe he doesn't want to marry me anymore."

Ruby made a small sound of sympathy, but I kept my tone practical. "Juliet, if Freddie is the kind of man who'd flee at the first sign of difficulty, then you're better off knowing now. But I don't think that's what's happening."

"No?" Juliet turned her hope-filled gaze to me.

"I think he's confused, perhaps even frightened. But not about you."

She sniffed and pressed a lacy handkerchief to her nose. "You're always so steady, Veronica. I wish I had your calm."

"It's practice," I said. "And tea and crumpets. Lots of it."

That earned a small, watery laugh, and she sat up a little straighter. "Actually, that sounds marvellous. My appetite has been up and down for weeks."

I gave her a moment to collect herself then pressed on. "As much as I'd love to soothe all your concerns, I came to ask you both about someone."

Juliet blinked. "Who would that be?"

"Angus," I said. "I'd like to know what you really think of him."

"Oh. He's helpful, I suppose." Juliet looked a touch confused. "I don't really think about him."

"Has he ever made you feel uncomfortable?" I asked. "Or overstepped his duties?"

Lady Sophia waved a hand. "He's staff. Not to be noticed unless the heating's failing, or the wine is warm. The staff makes one feel comfortable, not the opposite."

I focused on Juliet. "Nothing comes to mind about him?"

She shook her head. "As Sophia said, he does his job. I have no complaints, and I've only heard other family members say good things about him."

"What about Constance?" I asked. "Did she have concerns about Angus?"

Juliet sat upright. "Why are you so focused on Angus?"

"I'm exploring a possibility."

Her mouth dropped open. "Oh! You don't think he's our killer, do you?"

"He's not your man," Lady Sophia said with the assured air of someone who'd already solved the murder. "If anyone complained about anything, it would have been Constance to Angus. And it would have been complaints about Juliet, since she ran the woman ragged."

"Ignore everything Sophia says." Juliet glared at Lady Sophia. "If you keep talking like that, you'll no longer be my matron of honour."

"I will happily step back from that role. I despise the colour of the dresses," Lady Sophia said. "Pink is so last season."

"They are not pink. They're coral haze."

"Returning to Angus." I shared a look of exasperation with Ruby. "Lady Sophia, why are you so sure he's not the killer?"

"The thought of this wedding gives me a blinding headache," she said. "I've been through that palaver myself, and I wouldn't wish it on my worst enemy. Angus shared that sentiment."

"You horror! You make my wedding sound like a war zone." Juliet stood from her seat and tossed her handkerchief aside. "It'll be the very best day of my entire life. I'll be a happily married woman. My life will be complete."

"If that's your idea of happiness, then you have a sadly narrow view of this world," Lady Sophia said.

"That's it! You're no longer my matron of honour." Rage coloured Juliet's cheeks, and she clenched her hands. "If it weren't blowing a blizzard outside, I'd insist you leave immediately."

"Ladies, please! I'm attempting to solve a murder," I said. "A little decorum."

Juliet pouted. Lady Sophia ignored me.

"Lady Sophia, it sounds as if you spoke to Angus about the wedding," I said. "How is that possible, since you informed me that you had nothing to do with the help?"

She lifted a thin brow, entirely unrepentant. "Oh, come now, Miss Vale, must I account for every stray word I toss over a teacup? One doesn't require an engraved invitation to converse with the help, particularly when in need of entertainment."

"Angus entertained you?" Ruby asked.

"He was surprisingly diverting when I required stimulation. And I'm sure you will both agree that his face is quite a delight."

"You are fond of our estate manager?" Juliet almost squeaked the words. "That is entirely inappropriate."

"As if I'd belittle myself in such a manner," Lady Sophia remarked. "But the man has a curious turn of phrase. He's rough around the edges, naturally, but not without his charms. And I can only endure so many wedding fittings and recitations about seating charts before seeking a reprieve."

Juliet, red-cheeked and huffing, flung her hands in the air. "I've had quite enough of everyone implying that my wedding is trivial." She flounced from the room in a flurry of indignation.

"Oh dear. Have I upset her again? One wonders why Juliet is so prone to emotional outbursts. At least, I wonder. How about you, ladies?" Without waiting for an answer, Lady Sophia stood and sauntered away with feline grace, seemingly satisfied at upsetting Juliet again.

Ruby let out a slow breath. "Do you think she enjoys it?"

"Which part?" I asked. "Rattling Juliet or misleading me?"

"Both."

"Lady Sophia is clever, I'll give her that. Too clever to be so careless with her words unless she wanted us to hear them."

Ruby's brow furrowed. "That bit about Angus being charming... it was odd, wasn't it?"

"Highly."

Benji gave a soft snort, as though unimpressed by the entire exchange.

"You don't think..." Ruby lowered her voice and leaned closer. "Lady Sophia isn't involved with him romantically, is she?"

"She thrives on attention and is easily bored. Maybe she thought a flirtation with the rugged Scotsman would liven things up." I tilted my head, considering it. "We've seen no evidence of it, though. No shared glances. No inside jokes. Nothing to show any fondness."

"That doesn't mean it isn't happening," Ruby said. "Lady Sophia would be careful, wouldn't she? Despite being divorced, she has a reputation to maintain."

"If Constance learned about a relationship, that's another motive for needing to silence her."

"This won't do! We're collecting more motives than suspects," Ruby said.

"And we're no closer to understanding what Angus was hiding or what Constance had over him. If anything."

"She was meant to make this wedding run smoothly," Ruby said. "Instead, her murder has left a trail of secrets we keep tripping over."

"Let's hope we trip over the truth soon, before someone else winds up dead."

Chapter 18

We'd taken a few hours away from the rest of the party to mull over everything we'd learned about our remaining suspects. The discussion had involved several pots of strong tea and some delicious rectangular dark chocolate biscuits with a chocolate buttercream filling, which Ruby had snuck out of the kitchen.

The drawing room we'd tucked ourselves in was one of the cosier spaces in the castle, away from the more formal chambers and grand halls. A fire crackled in the hearth, the flames low and steady, casting flickers of orange and gold across the rug.

We occupied a pair of armchairs close to the grate, and Benji happily sprawled between them, his nose twitching as he dozed. Heavy damask curtains framed the windows, and the scent of tea and wood-smoke lingered in the air.

Ruby moved over and perched on the arm of my chair, toasting her stockinged feet by the fire, a cup of tea balanced precariously on her knee. "So, we're agreed. Angus had both an opportunity and a motive. If he was kissing Constance one minute and being slapped the next, and then to top that, she uncovered some misdeed, he'd have every reason to silence her."

"And the information from Gregor about Angus going cold on Constance suggested he nursed more than bruised pride," I said.

Ruby sighed. "Why are the handsome ones always such rotters?"

I glanced up at her. "Jacob isn't a rotter."

"Oh, you understand my meaning. A handsome face and a firm jawline allow them to get away with so much. I quite declare, you grabbed the last kind-hearted fellow left in this land who has a fine face."

"You'll find a decent sort. But perhaps look less at how handsome they are and more at their actions to determine their true character."

"That sounds terribly dull."

From down the corridor came a sudden sound that made us sit upright.

I stared at Ruby. "Was that the telephone?"

Ruby blinked. "They won't have made any repairs in this weather, surely."

We both stood, Benji lifting his head, ears perked. I crossed the floor with swift strides, Ruby hurrying to keep up, and we dashed into the hallway and towards the still ringing telephone.

We weren't the first to arrive. Juliet was just swooping up the receiver, Freddie and Lady Sophia close behind her, all looking surprised.

"I thought you said the telephone wasn't working?" Lady Sophia shot an accusatory glare at Juliet.

"It must be the police!" Juliet shushed her in a most unladylike manner as she clutched the receiver with one hand and pressed the other over her ear. "Yes, hello! Are you calling about our incident? Do you know that someone has died?"

Lady Sophia loomed beside her. "Give it here. You're being vague."

Freddie hovered awkwardly at Juliet's other side. "Be clear on what happened, my love, and that the body is still here. If the chap Gregor spoke to didn't believe him, he may not have passed on the message."

"I'm trying, but you both keep talking. Hello? Are you still there? This connection is full of crackle," Juliet said.

"Say Constance was stabbed," Lady Sophia demanded. "That'll get them here quick as you like."

"Would everyone please stop shouting at me?" Juliet squeaked, clinging to the receiver. "Hello? Hello? Are you there? We need help. Send help."

"Whoever is on the other end of that telephone must wonder if they're in a nightmare," Ruby murmured. "You should take charge. Take the telephone before Lady Sophia uses it to assault Juliet."

"I'm content to sit out this family squabble," I said. "And Juliet is doing her best."

"We've had... oh, dear, it's rather complicated, but there's been a situation," Juliet stammered.

Lady Sophia grabbed for the receiver. "I'll do it."

Juliet twisted away. "Stop interfering!"

Freddie tried to smooth things over by adjusting the cord, which promptly knocked the earpiece askew.

"Give it to someone with sense in their head!" Lady Sophia held out a hand.

"I have sense! All you have is a spiteful tongue and no husband." Juliet glowered at her. "No, I'm not speaking to you. I am now, though! Someone has been murdered. Here. In Augustine Castle. Did you catch that? M.U.R.D.E.R.E.D!"

There was a long pause.

"At least instruct them to send the police," Lady Sophia said.

"It could be the police." Juliet jiggled the receiver several times. "Drat! They've gone. I don't know if they heard me at all. I could only catch every third word they said."

Lady Sophia succeeded in taking the telephone and listened before thumping it down with a disgusted sigh. "What a wasted opportunity."

"Who was it?" I asked.

Juliet shook her head, her eyes wide with frustration. "A man. That's all I know. His voice was muffled, and then the line went crackly. Perhaps it *was* the police, checking to ensure all was well."

"It could have been anyone," Ruby muttered to me.

Lady Sophia adjusted her hair. "Why must you always dither? You've been like that since you were a child. It's most vexing."

"You didn't help matters," Juliet snapped. "You flustered me, so I forgot myself."

"I was the only one trying to introduce clarity," Lady Sophia said. "If anyone's to blame for that disaster, it's you and your wretched nerves."

I stepped in. "That's enough. They may call back when the telephone line reconnects, or are already sending help."

"Do you think they heard me?" There was a hopeful tint in Juliet's tone.

"There's an excellent chance they did." I didn't feel confident that any of our communications via the telephone had been effective.

"But what if they don't send anyone?" Juliet said, her voice wobbling slightly. "What if they think it was a prank?"

"If they consider it a prank, that is their concern. We must carry on as we have been." My voice was steady. "And if they send someone, we'll be ready with everything we know."

Freddie looked towards the telephone, his brow furrowed. "It's odd, though, that it rang at all."

"I tried to reach the operator several times today and got nothing," Juliet insisted. "So has Angus."

"They'll be working on the lines by now," Freddie said with certainty in his voice. "They'll want us connected swiftly. Everyone in the area has such high regard for Augustine Castle."

A slight sneer crossed Lady Sophia's face. "That's what you think. Now, I have a question for Miss Vale."

"Go ahead." What barb was she intending to throw in my direction?

"I've been thinking, and you've forgotten someone in this investigation." Lady Sophia's attention shifted to Ruby. "Your charming shadow has thus far escaped your clever little interviews."

Ruby straightened beside me. "That's because I didn't murder anyone."

Lady Sophia gave a humourless laugh. "How convenient. But you weren't seated at the table when the murder took place, were you?"

"No, but I merely stepped out for a moment."

"How long of a moment?"

"Steady on," I protested. "Ruby had nothing to do with what happened to Constance."

"It's perfectly fine. I don't know Lady Sophia, so she has a right to be suspicious." Ruby tilted her chin. "I was away from the table for perhaps ten minutes. I needed to change my stocking, and I looked in on my daughter."

"Did anyone see you?" Lady Sophia asked.

"Grace was sleeping, and the nanny was out of the room," Ruby said.

Lady Sophia's mouth curled into a stiff smile. "Which means no one saw you. And yet, you've been exempt from Veronica's questions. How curious."

"I trust Ruby," I said evenly. "And she is much more than my shadow. Her insight is often pivotal in solving crimes we've encountered."

"Ah, there it is," Lady Sophia said. "Blind loyalty. How quaint. But if you're interrogating lifelong servants and aristocrats, it seems only fair to include your closest companion. Or do I sense unfairness? Perhaps you are conspiring together."

Ruby gave me a look and then turned to Lady Sophia. "Very well. Ask me anything. I have nothing to hide."

A gleeful expression tightened Lady Sophia's face. "Where were you precisely when Constance was killed?"

"As I already told you, in my room. Where else would I keep my stockings?"

"I noticed you speaking to Constance shortly before her death. What was the content of your conversation?"

"Mainly about the wedding," Ruby said. "And I invited her to join us for dinner."

"Did you have any cause to dislike Constance?" Lady Sophia asked.

"None," Ruby said. "She had a sharp mind, boundless tolerance, and she appeared unflappable. Much like someone else I know and hold in high regard." She glanced at me and winked.

Lady Sophia tapped a manicured nail on the telephone console. "It strikes me that you had ample reason to resent Constance."

Ruby settled her hands on her hips. "Why would I do that?"

"Oh, come now," Lady Sophia said, her tone syrupy with mock sympathy. "A young, ambitious woman with a career. Well-dressed. Assertive. Constance turned heads. That can be awfully grating when one's own prospects are so far behind them."

Ruby gave a short laugh. "You think I murdered Constance because I was jealous of her career?"

Lady Sophia's eyes gleamed. "Constance was a reminder that you're not the ingenue anymore. That your days of turning heads are fading. Add in your infant and your status as a tragic war widow, and most men won't even give you the time of day. And good ones are in such short supply since we sent so many men to fight and they never returned home."

I stepped in quickly as a flush of fury stained Ruby's neck. "Let's stay focused, shall we? And polite. I won't abide personal insults."

Lady Sophia turned to me, unbothered. "And then we have Angus to add to this tangled motive your friend has surrounded herself with. He's not a hard man to read, and I saw the way he looked at Constance. I'm sure no one will disagree that he was quite taken with her. Perhaps you noticed too, Miss Smythe, and you didn't care for it. Jealousy is such an unattractive quality."

Ruby pressed her lips together, and I had to admire her restraint.

"I've heard you mention more than once how handsome you consider Angus to be." Lady Sophia sneered slightly. "You've spent hours trailing after him, all smiles and clever remarks. Then along comes a woman with better hair and a waistline not ruined by a child, and suddenly you're invisible, like the grey-haired great-aunt with too many cats who smells of peppermint."

"That's enough," I said sharply.

Lady Sophia pressed on. "Perhaps you thought removing Constance would restore the attention you'd lost, and you'd find a man to plant your flag in."

Ruby gave her a flat look. "If I killed every woman prettier than me in this castle, you'd be the only one left."

That earned a snort from Freddie, which he quickly disguised as a cough when Lady Sophia glared at him.

Lady Sophia's smile returned, colder this time. "You deflect well. But a motive is a motive. Jealousy, spite, and a crushed opportunity. Those reasons for killing are older than any war story you could invent."

"I'm inventing nothing." Ruby spoke through gritted teeth.

Lady Sophia's eyes glittered with amusement, like a cat batting at a trapped bird. "What would your husband have thought about all of this?"

Chapter 19

Ruby blinked, struggling to keep her composure. "Show some respect. My husband is dead."

"Such a tragic loss. Remind me, which regiment was he in? I'm always fascinated by the tales of brave boys lost in the war," Lady Sophia said.

Ruby smoothed her hand over her skirt, her gaze dropping. "The Wiltshires."

The story she'd told ever since becoming an unmarried mother was usually delivered with a practiced sadness. Yet somehow, Lady Sophia knew something was amiss. If she weren't such a thoroughly unpleasant character, I'd enjoy puzzling through a case with her. Her mind was certainly sharp enough to bring down the villains.

"Heartbreaking," Lady Sophia murmured. "And yet you've done so well for yourself. No close family to assist, no obvious means of support, and yet here you are, travelling, mingling with the elite, and always dressed so beautifully. That is remarkable for a war widow."

Ruby gave her a thin smile. "I make the most of what I have."

"Indeed. And what you had, or what you could have had with Angus, Constance threatened." Lady Sophia's eyebrows flashed up. "You have no alibi, a mysterious past, and a close connection to the woman currently running this show. It's not unthinkable that you killed Constance and have the perfect friend to ensure you get away with it."

"You speak nonsense," Ruby said.

Lady Sophia turned to me, dismissing the conversation with a wave. "Well, Miss Vale? Are you satisfied with your friend's answers? Or would you delve deeper to see what secrets lie under the slightly faded but still lovely veneer?"

"I am more than content to testify that Ruby is innocent," I said, my voice cool. "Are you?"

"Not especially. But that's one of the many differences between us. I enjoy asking questions and learning the truth, while you only enjoy answers that suit your way of thinking," Lady Sophia said.

Freddie cleared his throat. "We're all innocent of any crime, so let's have less of this unpleasant debate. It's still early, but I'm already tired from all of this uncertainty. Hopefully, that was the police, and they will arrive soon and take control of this nasty business."

"We have a killer and a liar inside these castle walls," Lady Sophia said, turning to Juliet. "If it wasn't Ruby, then maybe you lied about the broken telephone to trap us and pick us off one by one."

Juliet made a tiny, indignant snort. "Now you really are being ridiculous. You must have slept badly. Perhaps you were up rifling through the office in the Thistle Inn."

"I slept soundly, but then my conscience is clear," Lady Sophia said. "I'm unable to say that about anyone else."

"Piffle! Explain why I would murder Constance?" Juliet asked.

"Because the thought of spending the rest of your life married to the bumbling Freddie sent you stumbling into madness," Lady Sophia said. "We've all seen the evidence in your regular theatrics."

"I'm a catch!" Freddie said. "And Juliet is no madder than I am."

Lady Sophia chuckled at that reply.

"You're the only mad one around here," Juliet said, her hands in fists and her cheeks red. "Take that all back, including what you said about Ruby, or I really will shove you into the snow and leave you to freeze."

"Who thinks that comment sounds like the ravings of an unhinged mind?" Lady Sophia crossed her arms over her chest. "If you'd come at *me* with a dagger, you wouldn't be standing."

"Ladies, we must find a way to a truce," Freddie said. "No one here is the killer. We all saw someone outside, so I vote we have a stranger stalking us."

"That hardly makes me feel better!" Juliet's eyes sparked fury as she focused on Lady Sophia.

"You'd prefer the killer to be inside the castle?" Lady Sophia smirked. "Is that because you know who it is, so you have nothing to be afraid of?"

Juliet and Lady Sophia glared icily at each other, neither desiring to relent.

Angus stepped into the hallway, clearing his throat to announce himself. "If I may interrupt. Let's get back into the warmth. I've had Gregor help with banking the fires, and I can fix us some afternoon tea and cake."

That broke the tension, and we all agreed tea and cake would be just the ticket. I was particularly eager to find some sustenance, since we'd missed lunch to focus on the suspects.

Ruby and I peeled away from the others, slipping into the quiet of the library where the only eyes watching us were from the dour portraits of long-dead ancestors.

Benji followed us and settled next to me. I ran a hand over his ears, grateful for the grounding comfort of warm fur and familiar company.

Ruby folded her arms and stared at the paintings. "If Lady Sophia could have slapped me with a glove and challenged me to pistols at dawn, she would have. She sounded so convinced that I murdered Constance."

"Lady Sophia was being deliberately vexing and casting suspicion around like confetti in the hope no one would look too closely at her," I said.

Ruby gave a half-smile. "I feel guilty, and I've done nothing dishonest. Well, my tiny lie about my husband never feels pleasant, but that's the size of my deceit."

"Lady Sophia is pointing fingers too freely," I said. "Either she's protecting someone or she's terrified we'll return to her when we find evidence of her guilt."

"I believe she's simply bored and wants to see what happens when she kicks the hornet's nest," Ruby muttered. "The way she spoke about my husband... well, I felt the shame bubble up and almost wanted to tell everyone the truth."

"That story is to protect you. It's society's shame, not yours," I reminded her.

"I know! But I feel dreadful every time I tell the tale." She sighed. "Let's focus on solving this puzzle so I can stop feeling so dreadful. Who should we focus on? Angus or Lady Sophia?"

"We can't rule out Angus. We have motive, a potential grudge, and his convenient dirk knowledge. But with Lady Sophia flinging suspicion around, she's moving up the list."

Hurried footsteps echoed from the far end of the main hallway, and I glanced up just in time to see Juliet flit past the open door, her head down and her pace quick.

Ruby arched a brow. "Who was that?"

"Juliet. And she looked like she was fleeing a crime scene," I murmured, already on my feet and following.

Benji trotted after me, with Ruby catching up as we trailed Juliet around the corner and past the kitchen doors. She continued to the end of the hallway and slipped into the dried goods and tins pantry.

I frowned. The kitchen held all the fresh ingredients, so if Juliet was too hungry to wait for tea and cake to be served, she'd have gone in there to find something.

I pressed a finger to my lips, and Ruby nodded. We crept forward and peeked inside the slightly open door.

Shelves of tins, sacks of flour, and preserves surrounded Juliet. She had a tin of golden syrup open and was dunking a large green pickle into it before shoving it into her mouth with alarming gusto and then groaning with pleasure.

We watched in silence for a few seconds before Ruby gently tugged me back.

"Perhaps we should leave her to it?" Ruby pressed her lips together, holding in a laugh.

"Pickles and syrup?" My mouth twisted. "What an odd combination."

"She's doing no harm. Let's return to the library and figure out whom to tackle next."

"Why are you both skulking here?"

We jumped at the haughty note in Lady Sophia's voice.

Juliet must have also heard because she yelped, and there was a clatter as a tin hit the stone floor. She poked her head out of the door. "Oh! Why are you spying on me?"

Lady Sophia sauntered closer. "The more pertinent question is why are you eating that odd combination again?"

"I'm eating nothing." Juliet looked at the leaking tin of syrup.

"Don't you ladies think it curious?" Lady Sophia asked as she stopped a short distance from the pantry.

"I... I was famished. I ate so little breakfast and was asleep when lunch was served." Juliet dabbed golden syrup off her chin. Her eyes narrowed. "I don't appreciate being followed."

"We meant no harm. We were just curious about where you were going," I said. "Is something the matter?"

"Of course! Everything is the matter. My wedding is in ruins, and there's a killer on the loose. Nothing is right about any of this." Juliet threw up a hand. "And now, I can't even have a moment's peace in my family home."

"If it's any comfort, I overindulge with cake when I'm overwhelmed," Ruby said.

"As your waistline declares," Lady Sophia said.

"Ruby has not long had a child," I snapped at her.

"Well then, this little mystery should be a doddle to deduce." Lady Sophia eyed the open jar of pickles.

Juliet sighed and gestured us into the pantry. Lady Sophia stopped by the door, refusing to enter.

"My stomach hasn't been right for weeks," Juliet finally said. "One minute, I can barely look at food, and the next, I'm ravenously hungry. And my taste buds have changed. I used to adore poached eggs and buttered toast, but the very idea of it turns my stomach. You hear of it, don't you? Brides with nervous stomachs."

"That's true," I said cautiously. "You say you've felt like this for several weeks?"

"It comes and goes," Juliet said. "When we were at dinner on the night Constance died, I felt terribly uncomfortable, so I excused myself to use the facilities. I said I'd gone to check on Angus, and I did for a few minutes, but then had to excuse myself. It's all rather embarrassing."

"You're fooling no one," Lady Sophia said.

"I'm not attempting any form of deception," Juliet said. "And why are you still here? Don't you have to put on your snowshoes? I was serious about not wanting you here. It's time you left before you poison anyone else's thoughts."

Lady Sophia waved an elegant hand in the air. "It's clearly escaped your notice, given your fragile mind, but this castle belongs to my family."

"We're of the same family," Juliet said.

"Yes, but I am older, not by many years, but I have a larger claim over these bricks. You'd do well to remember that before attempting to throw me out."

Juliet's clenched fists returned.

"Returning to your poor health," I said, "did anything trigger you feeling unwell?"

"I have been on an appallingly strict diet for this wedding," Juliet said. "I wondered if that caused it."

"Stop pussyfooting around," Lady Sophia said. "These wedding arrangements may have dragged on for years, but my dearest Juliet and Frederick have acted like a married couple for some time, in every sense of the word. This outcome was inevitable, since neither of them has the sense they were born with."

My gaze went to Juliet's stomach, which was carefully concealed by a fluted frill on her custom-made silk dress. "Oh! You're with child."

Chapter 20

Juliet's eyes widened with the horror of someone caught red-handed committing a crime. "I... I'm not. That's absurd!"

Lady Sophia let out a bark of laughter. "Oh, do stop with this nonsense. You've been hiding the scandal under those ugly ruffles for weeks."

Juliet's mouth opened and closed, and her rapidly blinking eyes turned to me.

"Is this true?" I gently took hold of her sticky hand.

"Freddie doesn't know!" she whispered at last. "And he can't know yet."

Ruby and I exchanged a look.

"You really should tell him," I said gently. "He adores you."

"I was going to," Juliet said, her voice trembling. "After the wedding. When things have settled."

"You mean, when you have a ring on your finger so he can't change his mind." Lady Sophia arched an eyebrow.

"It's not as if it's anyone's business but mine!" Juliet sank onto a wooden crate. "I don't want to trap Freddie. That was never my plan. We just... well, we got carried away."

"You're not the first woman this has happened to." Ruby knelt beside her, taking her other hand.

"I suppose you'll go running to Freddie now?" Juliet shot at Lady Sophia.

"Certainly not," she sniffed. "I thrive on scandal, not the consequences of it. And I've kept this secret for weeks, so why would I reveal it now?"

"You intend to hold it over my head." Juliet's eyes filled with tears. "You truly are wicked."

"When circumstances are reduced, ingenuity must shine." Lady Sophia glanced my way. "Isn't that correct?"

Neither Ruby nor I responded.

Lady Sophia offered a smile full of venom. "I'll leave you ladies to your domestic unravelling. All this talk of infants has quite exhausted me." She turned and glided from the pantry.

Juliet stared after her, colour rising high on her cheeks. "She's hateful! Utterly vile. If she weren't family, I'd never speak to her again."

"Lady Sophia has a talent for getting under the skin," Ruby said.

"She delights in it," Juliet snapped. "She always knows what to say to make me feel like a complete fool. And now she knows about my child, she'll use it against me the moment it suits her."

"Has anyone else discovered your situation?" I asked.

"No. No one." She looked at us. "Please, you can't tell anyone. I'll speak to Freddie, I will. But it has to be in my own time, and in my own way. Promise me you'll keep it to yourselves."

Ruby and I exchanged another glance.

I gave a quick nod. "You have my word."

"Mine too," Ruby said.

Juliet exhaled shakily, her shoulders drooping. "Thank you. With everything that's going on, I feel exhausted. I'm going to my room to rest." She stood and stepped past us, one hand pressed protectively to her stomach, and disappeared.

"Well," Ruby said after a few seconds had passed. "That was unexpected."

I gently nudged Benji's nose away from a storage bin. "This family is full of surprises."

"Juliet's secret won't stay hidden for long now that Lady Sophia knows."

"If Constance found out about the child before the wedding, she might have threatened to say something," I said. "That would have embarrassed Juliet. Or worse, caused Freddie to call the whole thing off."

Ruby's brows lifted. "Juliet killed Constance to keep her quiet about her child?"

"Or Constance asked for something to maintain her silence," I said. "Constance would have noticed what Juliet was eating, how her shape changed at the dress fittings, and when she rested."

"Blackmail! That's a poor show. Constance must have made a decent living from being involved in such high society weddings," Ruby said. "But given Juliet's delicate condition, would she have committed the crime? If she feels anything like me when I was with child, she'd barely be able to get out of bed some days."

"Juliet is capable of more than she lets on. And she's always been ambitious," I said. "I recall an occasion in Sunday school when we had to create collages for a Harvest Festival church display. Juliet envied another girl's design, so she knocked a glass of water over it. It was ruined. She swore it was an accident, but I was never certain."

"If Constance had the power to ruin everything Juliet has spent two years preparing for, that's an excellent motive for murder."

I sighed. "I hate to think poorly of a friend, but this nudges Juliet up the list of suspects."

Ruby gave a slow nod. "We need to find Constance's notes or her diary. Anything that could prove she knew about the child."

"We could search her room," I said.

"Should we do it now?"

"After we've had tea and cake. People will be full and resting, so we'll be less likely to be disturbed." Besides, I was famished.

Ruby wrinkled her nose. "Assuming anyone has an appetite with all that's going on."

"Murder does dampen the mood. Although there is always room for cake."

After a delicious spread of hot crumpets, homemade fruitcake, and a huge tin of crumbly shortbread biscuits, which more than made up for the stilted conversation and sour looks that passed between the company, I made my excuses and headed upstairs with Ruby and Benji to undertake a little snooping.

We waited in my bedroom for five minutes, giving the remaining castle residents time to settle into their pursuits, then I inched open the door and listened intently for several seconds. There were no sounds of anyone else moving around.

I gestured for Ruby and Benji to follow, and we headed onto the landing. I'd taken off my shoes, and the thick carpet underfoot made it easy to move without making a sound.

We crept to Constance's bedroom, which was at the end of the corridor, checked once more that no one observed us, and snuck into the room, the squeak of the handle making me wince.

It had a similar layout to my bedroom, although the decoration was slightly less elaborate. There was an enormous wardrobe, a dressing table, a chest of drawers, two bedside cabinets with a single cup and saucer on one cabinet, and a double bed dominating the room.

I inspected the dressing table first but found nothing but a few cosmetics. I went to the bedside cabinets. They were empty. There was a pungent floral smell coming from the empty teacup. Perhaps Constance had a fancy for Earl Grey tea. It was too flowery for my tastebuds, but certain high society circles adored it.

"Benji's got something," Ruby called out softly.

Benji had stopped beside the wardrobe and rested a paw on it.

I headed over and inched open the door. I froze as a hinge creaked, and I held my breath.

When no one came to investigate the noise, I eased the door the rest of the way open. Several smart dresses hung inside, and there were two pairs of low-heeled shoes. There was also a small travel case inside the wardrobe.

I lifted it out and opened it. A net bag held undergarments, and a notebook was tucked into a compartment.

I pulled the notebook free just as Ruby hissed, "Footsteps! They're coming this way."

Benji gave a low growl, his ears pricking.

The tread was light and quick, not heavy enough to be a man, and they grew closer by the second.

"Wardrobe," I whispered, thrusting the notebook at Ruby.

"We won't both fit!" she whispered back, wild-eyed. "You take Benji in there. I'll find somewhere else to hide."

My gaze darted around. "The curtain!"

Ruby darted behind the heavy brocade curtain, disappearing into the folds. I ducked into the wardrobe with Benji, easing the door nearly shut behind me. He pressed close, his warm breath against my calf.

The bedroom door squeaked open a second later. From the crack in the wardrobe door, I could see only a pair of stockinged feet. The figure paused, and I held my breath.

The woman moved with purpose, gliding softly towards the dressing table. A few seconds of silence passed then came the faintest creak of a drawer being opened. Another pause. A click as it shut again.

She turned, and I heard soft steps on the rug. Then a long pause. Through the crack, I saw her feet shift slightly, as if she turned slowly, scanning the room.

Two male voices sounded faintly in the corridor. I recognised it was Lord Robert and Freddie. They grew ever closer. Were they coming in here too?

The woman searching the room skipped to the door, but she didn't leave. The voices passed, and another few seconds shifted before the door clicked softly shut.

I stayed frozen in place with Benji for a full minute. Finally, I edged the wardrobe open and stepped out, Benji following. Ruby slipped from the curtain a second later.

"Did you see who it was?" she whispered.

"No. Only her feet," I said. "It was definitely a woman. She wore good quality stockings."

"I was too scared to peek in case the curtain moved," Ruby said. "Do you think she took anything?"

"Whoever it was, they were looking for something." I pointed at the notebook. "Maybe this."

Ruby grinned. "But we got here first. Let's see what secrets Constance didn't take to her grave."

We moved to the window, where a stark, bright light from the heaps of snow made reading easier.

"It's notes about this castle," I said after browsing the pages for a moment.

"Constance must have done her research while organising the wedding." Ruby kept reading over my shoulder. "How odd. Constance did heaps of research on the castle's history."

"That's not relevant to the wedding," I said. "I understand her needing to know the castle layout and room sizes to ensure everything fit and guests had enough space, but the history of Augustine Castle shouldn't come into it."

"It's all here," Ruby said as I flipped through more pages. "Names of ancestors, who inherited what. Pages and pages of it. She could have been a history buff."

"It's possible, although the interest never arose when we spoke," I said.

Benji's whine drew my attention. He was still by the small travel case, pawing at it.

"What else have you found?" I left Ruby reading the notebook and crouched beside Benji.

He nosed the travel case several times and then stared at me. His finely tuned nose must have alerted him to something I'd missed.

I checked the case again, lifting the undergarments and moving everything carefully. In a pouch, I found a cosmetics bag, which I extracted and opened.

"Oh, my goodness," I whispered. Rather than the usual toothpaste and face cloth, I stared at enormous rolls of banknotes.

Chapter 21

"Why would Constance have all that money?" Ruby stared at the notes I'd laid out on the floor.

"A society hostess of this calibre must receive a fair wage, but not this much," I said.

"Perhaps it's for wedding items," Ruby said. "It could be a kitty for last-minute bits and bobs. Maybe Juliet gave it to her because she keeps wanting more things purchased."

"Everything has been ordered and delivered ahead of time." I shook my head. "And suppliers would send an invoice or be paid in advance with a cheque."

"Could Constance have brought the money with her?" Ruby asked.

"There's nothing to spend it on around these parts," I said. "And why so much?"

"If Constance didn't bring it with her and Juliet didn't provide her with it as part of the wedding, it means someone in our party gave it to her," Ruby said. "A blackmail payment, perhaps?"

"You could be right. Payment in cash suggests whoever gave Constance this money didn't want it traced back to them," I said.

We stared at the money in silence.

"What should we do with it?" Ruby finally asked.

"We have to leave everything where we found it," I said. "The notebook and the money. When the police arrive, this could be important."

"Or we set the money on the table at dinner," Ruby said. "See everyone's reaction. Whoever gave Constance this money won't be able to hide their surprise."

"That action would reveal we were snooping," I pointed out.

"We need to snoop!" Ruby said. "We have to find out who murdered Constance. That could have been her killer sneaking in to recoup her money."

"There are only two women in this castle apart from us," I said.

"Lady Sophia and Juliet. Which neatly narrows our suspects to two." Ruby brushed a finger over the money. "We could confront them separately, see what information comes out."

"I like that plan. Let's set things back in place and find our targets," I said.

We tucked the notebook and money back into Constance's case, exactly as we'd found them, and slipped out of the room unseen.

The plan was simple. Get Lady Sophia and Juliet on their own, away from prying eyes. Ask the right questions. Watch their faces. Gauge their lies.

But the afternoon had other plans.

Lady Sophia was a wraith that glided from room to room, with someone always at her elbow or hanging off her words, despite my requesting her company more than once and receiving a dismissal or a promise of later.

Juliet, meanwhile, clung to Freddie like an amorous barnacle, all giggles and bright eyes. If she had a care in the world, she hid it beneath a veil of soon-to-be marital glee.

When dinner arrived a few hours later, I was almost beyond civility. Every move I'd made was blocked. And it had been the same experience for Ruby.

Our meal passed in a blur of overcooked lamb, dry potatoes, and clinking cutlery. There'd been no opportunity to converse privately with either target, and our general dinner conversation remained overly formal, as if we were all meeting for the first time. It proved everyone was on edge, wondering what the killer would do next.

I watched everyone carefully. Lady Sophia held court at the head of the table, making caustic observations and casting long, appraising looks. Beside her, Lord Robert downed two glasses of claret and made a show of swirling a third.

Across from me, Ruby caught my eye and gave a tiny shake of her head. There was still no opportunity to tangle with our targets, and my patience was wearing thin. I didn't want another night of sleeping in the same building as a killer.

As Angus cleared the last course and announced coffee, I rose from the table with every intention of tackling Lady Sophia, determined to snatch five uninterrupted minutes.

"Miss Vale!" Freddie popped up like a jack-in-the-box, holding out a small silver tin. "May I tempt you to some Scottish tablet? A wonderful local company makes it. The recipe is a secret they refuse to share, but it is simply divine. It has a crumbly, caramelised consistency."

"Later, thank you," I said, side-stepping him.

"Do have some," he insisted, flipping the lid open. "I can never stop at one piece. I was even considering purchasing the company so I'd have an endless supply of the stuff."

Lady Sophia swept past me with her coffee cup in hand. Drat.

As I turned to follow her, Lord Robert loomed at my elbow. "That was a fine supper," he said, patting his stomach. "I noticed you ate little. I suppose you need to keep yourself in tip-top form."

"Why would I need to do that?" My gaze flicked to Lord Robert.

His eyes went to my bare ring finger. "Don't worry, my dear. There will be a fine governess role for you on some estate. You have a sharp mind, although you'll need to watch that tongue of yours if you're to maintain any position of note."

My desire to say many a rude slight to Lord Robert faded as Lady Sophia disappeared from view. "Excuse me."

"Miss Vale." Angus appeared beside us with surprising stealth, holding a folded handkerchief. "I believe this is yours. I found it beneath your seat."

I blinked at him. "No. I don't carry that kind of handkerchief."

Between Lord Robert's posturing and Angus's intervention, Lady Sophia had too good of a head start on me, so I diverted to Juliet, who was still in the room, only to be blocked once more by Freddie, now waving a games box.

"Let's have a few rounds of charades, shall we?" he said, beaming. "It might raise the spirits. Dinner was dreadfully glum, and we can't permit this mood to sour things any further."

"I've no talent for acting," I said.

"Nonsense. You've got a fine, expressive face. Just what we need."

"I have been perfecting my scowl this evening," I muttered under my breath.

Juliet hurried over, tucked her hand around Freddie's elbow, and murmured something that made him laugh before they headed off together to set up.

Ruby joined me, handing me a coffee. "Luck is not on our side. They're like eels in a bucket. Every time you reach for one, it slips away."

"Yes," I said grimly. "And now we must watch them play charades. But I refuse to take part. It'll only cause a distraction."

"Truly the greatest indignity yet." Ruby grinned. "I may have a turn. We need a break from hunting our slippery killer, and I do enjoy a good game. I'm a whizz with anything to do with music. At the very least, we should sit with them."

Once we were settled in the games room, a roaring fire going, and coffee and brandy liberally dispensed, Juliet threw herself into the game with far more enthusiasm than I'd anticipated, fluttering across the room and miming what might have been a chicken laying an egg.

Lady Sophia declared it "tragically indecent," while Lord Robert guessed *Fanny Hill* three times in a row, despite being told it wasn't a scandalous novel.

"She's doing *The Importance of Being Earnest*," Freddie bellowed, standing on a footstool for no reason.

"I am not!" Juliet flapped her arms some more. "No one? Oh, I give up. It was *Wuthering Heights*. Honestly, Freddie, you should have known that."

"This is glorious." Ruby turned her head, wiping her eyes as she laughed. Even Benji, curled beside my chair, gave a huff that might have passed for amusement.

I allowed myself the smallest of smiles. The scene had a strange charm, like watching a tipsy aristocracy play at being normal, but my mind never left the task at hand. I watched Juliet between every round, timing her laughter, noting her forced smiles. Something was gnawing at her, even as she clapped and guessed along with the others. Was it the desire to reclaim the money blackmailed from her or the guilt she felt for plunging in the blade? Perhaps both.

Finally, when Freddie launched into an overlong impression of a cow being abducted by a farmer, I saw my opening.

Juliet had slipped to the side table for a drink, her back to the firelight. I rose from my chair and crossed the rug quickly, glass in hand.

"Juliet," I whispered. "May I have a moment?"

She looked up, her eyes wary. "Now? It's my turn next."

"Just a quick word. About Constance—"

There was a sharp *pop*, and we were plunged into darkness.

Chapter 22

A chorus of surprised exclamations echoed around us as our startled faces glowed in the firelight.

"Good heavens!" Lady Sophia cried out. "Which ninny turned off the light?"

"I think I just sat on someone!" Lord Robert yelped. "My apologies, whoever that was."

"Everybody stay still while your eyes adjust," I said. "And someone find candles."

"It must be the snow," Freddie said in the gloom. "I'm surprised this hasn't already happened."

Benji leaned against my leg and softly whined.

"There's nothing to worry about," I murmured to him, my gaze darting around as I tried to pick out anyone skulking about.

There was a thump and a muttered curse, then the door opened. Angus stood in the gloomy gap. "All is well. There must be an issue with the electrics. I'll go see what's happened and bring in some lamps."

Before he could disappear, Lady Sophia swept up beside him with unexpected speed. "You'll need someone with sense to accompany you."

He nodded swiftly. The door banged shut behind them, and the flames sputtered and danced from the sudden gust of air, casting flickering shadows across the room.

In the wavering gloom, I noticed Juliet was back beside Freddie, clutching his arm. Was she avoiding me? She certainly didn't seem eager to speak with me, although perhaps that was more to do with the secret about her child rather than the murder.

"Blasted modern nonsense," Lord Robert grumbled, jabbing at the fire with an iron poker. "You never had this trouble with candles. They're reliable and timeless. No wires to go wrong, you see."

"And you only had to spend an hour extinguishing them before bed and then scrub the soot off the walls," Ruby murmured to me. "Although naturally, Lord Robert would never think of the servants."

"Electricity also means you don't accidentally set your curtains ablaze while reading a novel in bed," I whispered.

"The wiring in this place is a fright. It was probably strung up in haste and never inspected," Lord Robert continued. "Give me a good beeswax taper any day."

Juliet gave a tight sigh. "Does anyone else find the lack of light unnerving? What if someone did this? They want to unnerve us. Perhaps... even try again."

"Another murder?" Lord Robert snorted. "They'd be a fool to try anything while we're together. The killer would be better off tackling us one by one."

Juliet shuddered. "It's possible, though, isn't it?"

Angus burst through the door again, causing Juliet to squeak, snow clinging to his shoulders and hair, his boots leaving a trail of slush across the floor. Lady Sophia was behind him, her cheeks flushed from the cold, and her eyes gleaming with something between indignation and excitement.

"There's someone outside!" Angus's voice was urgent. "A big brute. Crouched but moving fast. I saw him by the old gate behind the kitchens when I was collecting lamps from the storeroom."

Everyone in the room fell still.

I stepped forward. "You're certain it was a person?"

"As certain as I can be with the blasted snow whipping in my face," he said. "He wasn't small."

Lady Sophia removed her gloves. "I saw him too. Just a glimpse."

"It was probably some poor fool from the village checking the lines," Lord Robert said. "Perhaps he's the buffoon who caused the problem we find ourselves in. They send out these types with barely any education and less sense, and what do you expect will happen?"

"No one's checking anything in this weather," Angus said. "The snow has started up again, and there's a vicious wind."

I crossed to the window and wiped away the mist with my sleeve. Snow lashed the glass in thick curtains, the courtyard little more than a blur of white and shadow. I saw no movement, but the wind howled through a crack like a warning.

"Where are the lamps and candles?" Freddie asked. "We need light! Juliet is trembling with terror."

Angus drew in a shaky breath. "I dropped them when I saw the figure. I'll go back."

"You can't go back out there alone," I said. "If someone's prowling the estate, we need a plan to protect ourselves."

"I could fetch the guns," Angus said.

"No guns!" I said. "I'll join you with Benji. He'll alert us to any trouble."

Angus hesitated then gave a single nod.

We left Ruby with strict instructions to bar the door behind us. As the front door groaned open, a gust of freezing wind hurled itself through the opening like a beast uncaged.

Benji pressed against my leg, his eyes fixed on the shifting shadows beyond the steps.

"Stay close," I murmured, stepping into the night.

Angus led the way. The snow had crusted over with ice, crunching noisily beneath our boots as we crossed the path to the storage shed near the west wing.

Branches bent under the weight of snow, creaking in the wind, and casting long, skeletal shadows across the ground. Something rustled to our left. Perhaps it was only a hare, but I didn't risk assuming.

Benji halted, his body taut.

"What is it?" I whispered, following his line of sight.

I saw nothing. Just the black beyond the orchard. But the hair on my neck stood up all the same.

Angus fumbled with the shed door before yanking it open to reveal lamps, wicks, and candles. He exhaled. "Thank God it's all dry."

I kept my attention on the tree line. "Gather what you can and give me plenty, too. Then let's get back inside."

The snow muffled everything as the wind whistled around, giving me a sense of creeping unease that someone was watching.

Benji growled again, louder this time.

"Go," I said. "Quickly!"

We hurried back, arms laden with supplies. I dared a glance over my shoulder. Nothing moved. But I couldn't shake the feeling that someone had just slipped out of sight.

Perhaps I'd been wrong all this time, and a dangerous stranger was lurking close by.

I tapped on the door, and Ruby instantly pulled it open, ushered us in, and then fixed the heavy bolt into place.

Fifteen minutes later, all the doors were checked, and we had lamps on tables in the room and a plentiful supply of candles and matches. We were all taking turns looking out the windows for the mysterious intruder.

"This power cut won't be fixed quickly." Angus stood by the window, watching as the blizzard continued. "But at least there's no sign of the troublemaker."

"They won't be able to get inside," Freddie said. "Not without alerting us."

Angus nodded. "May I suggest we call it a night? There's little we can do without power."

"We need to keep watch over the Thistle Inn office," I reminded everyone. "We can't risk a repeat of last night."

"No one will be interested in snooping in there again," Lady Sophia said.

"If they didn't find what they were looking for, they could return," I said.

"I'll take turns keeping watch with Gregor," Angus said. "We'll make sure the room remains secure until the police arrive."

Was that the correct course of action? Neither Angus nor Gregor had solid alibis, and Angus was near the top of the suspect list. Did I trust them?

"You can rely on us," Angus said, noticing my hesitation. "And you're welcome to take a turn, too, if it'll set your mind to rest."

"I will," I said. "I don't mind guarding the room with Benji."

"I'll take a shift, too," Ruby said. "With everything that's going on, I won't be able to sleep, so I'll make myself useful."

"Count me out." Lady Sophia was already heading towards the door, accompanied by Lord Robert. "I intend to have an excellent night's sleep."

After spending a few minutes with Angus and Gregor deciding how to split our time, we all turned in. Angus would take the first shift, followed by Gregor. Ruby was next, and I had the dawn shift. That was ideal because it gave us plenty of time to snoop around.

We waited in my room for half an hour, giving the castle guests time to settle, nestled on the bed with Benji.

"I can't imagine anyone will sleep easily tonight," I said.

"I know I won't," Ruby said. "I checked in on Grace earlier, and she seems to be the only one unaffected by all this nasty murder business."

"Lucky Grace. We'll share a room," I said. "We can top and tail and have Benji in between us."

"That will be snug," Ruby said with a grin. "I'm game if you are."

"Before we sleep, let's have a wander. We need to ensure no one is meddling in matters that don't concern them."

After removing our shoes so we could tiptoe around undetected, we'd only made it a few steps along the landing when quiet voices floated up the stairs.

"That's Angus!" Ruby whispered. "I recognise the accent."

A soft, feminine laugh drifted up next.

Ruby's eyes widened. "Whoever could that be?"

We crept to the top of the stairs and peered into the shadows below. A slender arc of torchlight glowed softly across the floor, the narrow beam held by Angus, though it barely reached the walls. He wasn't guarding the Thistle Inn as instructed. Instead, he was in conversation with Lady Sophia. Or rather, Lady Sophia was in conversation with him.

She stood close, just a little too close for a casual heart-to-heart. One hand rested lightly on his forearm, her other gesturing animatedly as she spoke. Her body angled towards him in a posture of quiet confidence. Her smile was faint but unmistakably there in the torchlight.

Angus, in contrast, was stiff as an iron gate. He kept both feet planted and his shoulders tense, barely moving except for the slow tilt of his head as he listened. He nodded once, said something low in return, but his hands never left the torch. His gaze didn't waver from hers, but it wasn't fondness I saw there. It was wariness.

"She's buttering Angus up," Ruby murmured beside me.

"Or convincing him to do something," I whispered. "Whatever it is, he's not buying it."

Lady Sophia leaned in slightly. Her fingers gave his sleeve a gentle pat, a fleeting touch meant to reassure or seduce.

Angus flinched, and the torch dipped as if his grip had loosened for a second. Then he straightened, pulling his arm back politely but firmly.

Lady Sophia didn't seem offended. If anything, she looked pleased, as though the entire exchange had gone exactly as planned. Then she leaned forward and pressed a kiss to his lips.

Ruby gave a soft gasp, and I quickly tugged her away before they spotted us.

She drew in several sharp, swift breaths. "What a scandal!"

"It's not such a scandal, although it is a surprise," I whispered.

"The lady and the hired help. Indeed, it is a scandal."

"Lady Sophia is unattached, and there's no wedding ring on Angus's finger," I said. "He told me he lives alone."

"But Lady Sophia is a snob," Ruby whispered in an excited tone. "She won't want her society friends in London hearing about this dalliance."

"They won't hear about it from me." I arched an eyebrow.

Ruby sighed. "I won't gossip! But so much for her being high and mighty if she's fraternising with Angus. Didn't she say something about ignoring the staff unless they did something wrong?"

"When there's a handsome face involved, people's sensibilities get turned around," I said with a knowing look in Ruby's direction.

She gently swatted me. "There's no need to get personal. We should get closer and listen. They could be discussing how to get away with murder."

A tinkle of laughter drifted up the stairs.

"Or they're conspiring to hide evidence," Ruby persisted.

I hesitated. "They're not working together. Angus is clearly uncomfortable."

"Maybe not anymore, but Lady Sophia lied about how well she knew Angus. Perhaps their affair soured after she convinced him to murder Constance, which is why he's so uneasy."

"He was the besotted lover, and Lady Sophia twisted him around her elegant finger?" I queried.

"Yes! She ordered him to stab Constance, and he obeyed, but now regrets it. Perhaps he wants to confess, but Lady Sophia is convincing him not to because it would implicate her."

More laughter sounded. If they were discussing heinous matters, they must find murder highly amusing.

I peeked over the banister. Lady Sophia leaned in again and reached out to straighten Angus's lapel. The intimate gesture sent his spine rigid, and he shifted his weight from one foot to the other.

"She's playing Angus," I whispered as Ruby joined me. "And he doesn't like the game."

Lady Sophia tilted her head in that theatrical way she had when toying with someone. Her hand lingered on his arm as she leaned in once more, and her lips brushed his cheek. Then she turned and glided away.

Angus exhaled, remaining by the wall and staring at the closed door she'd vanished through. One hand came up to rub his jaw. Then he crossed his arms and dropped his gaze to the flagstones, his shoulders sagging.

"He's rattled," I murmured.

"Lady Sophia rattles all of us," Ruby whispered.

Below us, Angus turned and trudged towards the Thistle Inn, his footsteps heavy.

We waited until his steps faded before retreating to my room.

Ruby sank onto the edge of the bed, her brow drawn in thought. "Well, if we didn't have enough secrets to uncover, we've just added another one."

"This castle is full of them." I pulled aside the curtain. The snow continued to fall, soft and relentless. A glance at the clock told me Ruby had only a few hours before it was her turn to watch over the Thistle Inn. "Let's try to sleep."

Ruby yawned, already sliding beneath the blankets. "Despite all the excitement, I might catch forty winks."

I extinguished the lamp and joined her, my mind spinning with possibilities as the shadows stretched longer across the ceiling.

Another storm was coming, and it had nothing to do with the inclement weather.

Chapter 23

"I'm happy to see us all here this morning." Freddie raised his cup as he stood from the table. "There were no problems overnight?"

"No one bothered me while I stood guard," Angus said.

We'd invited him to join us for breakfast, along with Gregor, since it seemed unfair to segregate them in their lodgings after the previous evening's adventures.

"The same here." I briefly considered grilling Angus about Lady Sophia's late-night visit, but that would give the game away.

Ruby nodded, her mouth full of toast.

"And what of Angus and Sophia's odd sighting?" Freddie asked. "Is there any clarity after sleeping on things? Was anyone else plagued by strange sightings in the dark?"

"I don't think there was much sleeping going on last night," Ruby whispered to me.

Angus reached for another slice of toast. "Whatever it was out there, I'm convinced it wasn't a trick of light and shadow."

"Nor the snow," Lady Sophia added, stirring her tea. "I'm not prone to hysterics, and there was definitely someone out there when we went to collect lamps."

Juliet clutched her teacup. "I knew it! There's a lunatic out there, creeping around in the dark. We need the police here this instant! Why aren't they here?"

"As soon as the telephone works, we'll contact them for an update," I said. "I checked first thing, and there wasn't so much as a crackle on the line."

"You're so calm about it all," Juliet said. "What if they do more harm while we wait? The police could arrive and find nothing but frozen corpses."

"How dreadfully morbid," Lady Sophia murmured.

"No one tried to break in last night," I said calmly.

"That we know of," Juliet said. "Did someone check all the doors and windows again?"

Gregor cleared his throat. "I had the same worries, so I took my gun and checked the grounds just after dawn. I looked everywhere and then inspected the entrances. No one bothered you during the night."

"Good man," Angus said.

Gregor nodded. "I'm just doing my job. I looked around the courtyard, the old stables, and along the edge of the forest path. There was nothing. No footprints, and no sign of anyone but us."

"Could the wind have covered their tracks with the fresh snow?" Ruby asked.

Gregor gave a small shrug. "Possibly. But if they lingered out there more than a few minutes, I'd have found something."

Angus nodded. "We can rely on Gregor."

Juliet paled. "So either they were quick or..."

"Or never left at all," Lady Sophia supplied, dabbing at her lips with a napkin. "We might have an intruder making themselves quite at home inside these very walls. Perhaps they know a secret way into those cobwebbed tunnels that was overlooked by mistake or due to a deliberate omission."

That suggestion made Juliet gasp again.

"Let's not frighten ourselves for the fun of it." I kept my tone measured. Lady Sophia was prodding to cause trouble. "There'll be a logical explanation as to who was outside last night. We just haven't uncovered it yet."

Angus's brow furrowed. "Whoever it was, they were fast and kept low to the ground, like they were hunching to avoid being noticed."

"The chap must have heard you go outside," Freddie said. "Perhaps they were near a window or seeking warmth in the old stables. You scared them off. Whoever it is, they must have a hardy constitution to withstand such frightful conditions."

As if to prove a point, the wind howled around the castle, and a pile of snow whipped up into a whirl close to the window.

"If this keeps up, the snow will cover the castle and we'll never be found." Freddie finished his tea and moved to a grand window, peering outside.

I assessed the suspects while they chatted about the inclement weather, all seeming grateful to sidle around the topic of murder, then set down my fork, fed Benji a bacon rind, and joined Freddie at the window.

He nodded at me. "Did you have any bright ideas overnight?"

"One or two," I said. "I want to ask you a question."

"Go ahead. I'm an open book. Juliet tells me I talk too much. My doctor says it's because of my nervous disposition. I can't imagine what he's blathering on about."

"It's a delicate matter. Money," I said.

"Oh! You're not after a loan, are you?" Freddie laughed. "I don't suppose a female journalist gets paid much. You do get some sort of wage, don't you? I'm a little out of touch with such matters. I have a chap who deals with that side of things in the family business."

"I'm amply compensated for my time," I said. "But I'm interested in how you paid Constance."

Freddie looked a little startled. "She provided a bill of costs as they were incurred, and I settled them. She mentioned there would be a final bill after the wedding, but we've dealt with most of them. Why do you ask?"

"How did you pay her?"

He looked perplexed. "In the normal manner."

"Which would be?"

"A cheque. A deposit secured Constance's services, and after that, she requested regular funds for catering, flowers, and other wedding necessities. Juliet's parents set up a fund for our wedding, which I could access to ensure everything ran smoothly."

"You always paid by cheque?" I asked.

"Naturally. It's tidier."

"What are you two whispering about?" Juliet joined us, placing a possessive hand on Freddie's arm as if she feared I may seduce him while he had breakfast crumbs on his shirt.

"Money, of all things," Freddie replied. "Veronica was asking about wedding payments."

Juliet's eyes sparkled. "Are you thinking about your happy day? You won't have such extravagance as us, but if you save hard, you and Jacob can have a splendid wedding. I will give you some tips."

"Hardly!" The word came out like a punch. Why was everyone so obsessed with me marrying? Jacob and I ticked along quite nicely just as we were.

"Oh, well, then I'm no help to you, since I have no head for figures." Juliet lightly laughed. "I'll leave that to my clever husband once we're married."

"If we marry..." Freddie's voice trailed off.

Juliet bit her bottom lip. "I still want to marry you, but I worry everyone will think it's crass to go ahead after Constance's death. However, we really can't wait a moment longer."

"I agree." Concern filled Freddie's gaze. "You seemed determined to carry on no matter what. Has something changed your mind?"

"I was awake all night," Juliet said. "I had an upset stomach from overindulging, and all I could think about was Constance. People will say awful things if we marry so soon after her murder."

"It is an unfortunate turn of events." Freddie patted her hand. "But don't we deserve our happy day?"

"Will it be happy?" Juliet raised her chin to the window. "Thanks to the ghastly weather, barely anyone will be here! And we don't have the vicar to make things official. He won't make the journey. And without our guests, we won't be able to submit photographs to the society pages. No one will know we were married!"

"The people who matter will," I said.

Juliet sighed. "I knew a jinx had been placed on our wedding, and I know exactly who did it." Her gaze shot to Lady Sophia.

"If the wedding goes ahead, I'll find space for your photographs in the London Times. I could suggest a special section for your wedding," I said. "It will be an extra gift from me."

"Oh! That would be wonderful. You're an ace, Veronica. And I'm so glad you made it. Are we ... is everything right between us?" Her gaze dipped to her stomach. "I wanted to speak to you again, but the nonsense with the lights and then everything else overwhelmed me."

"Everything is perfect. And I'm happy to help." It wouldn't serve me to reveal Juliet's impending motherhood to anyone. "May I speak with you in private now since we didn't finish our conversation after the lights went out?"

Juliet glanced up at Freddie. "If Freddie can manage without me."

He smiled. "I'm already missing you, my love, but off you go."

Juliet turned to me. "Let's use the morning room."

We slipped away from the bustle of the breakfast table, leaving behind clinking china and murmured gossip, and ducked into a quiet room overlooking the courtyard. Juliet settled onto the settee with a rustle of skirts, her eyes watchful.

"Is this about... you know?" Her gaze flicked to her stomach again.

"No. It's about Constance," I said.

Juliet let out a small breath and sat back, shoulders sagging in relief. "Oh. Of course."

"Did she have an interest in the history of Augustine Castle?"

Juliet's brow furrowed. "She never mentioned it to me. Although she spent an awful lot of time in the library. I thought she was working, but on one occasion, I found some history books left open on the desk."

"Did Constance ever speak of your family? Or ask about the Augustine lineage?"

"She was always curious about my family," Juliet said with a faint frown. "I assumed it was a passing fancy, or she just wanted to appear interested in us."

"Do you know anything about her family? Are they well-to-do?" I asked.

"I wouldn't have thought so, but she never said much about her parents, but then I never thought to ask," Juliet said. "There wasn't any grand fortune, if that's what you're asking. Why?"

"No particular reason," I said.

"There must be a reason, or you wouldn't be peppering me with all these questions." Juliet tilted her head. "Do you think this has something to do with her death?"

"I don't know yet," I said truthfully.

Juliet went quiet, her fingers twisting the edge of her sleeve. "I thought you were about to tell me about some scandal. I mulled over your questions about Constance and Angus, attempting to determine any affection between them, but the chap flirts with everyone. He can't help it. A wink here, a smile there.

Half the girls in the nearby village think he's in love with them."

"But none have won Angus's heart?" I asked.

"Not that I know of." She leaned forward slightly. "He's always careful. I think he knows the power he has and does his best not to misuse it. I blame the kilts."

"It had an interesting effect on Ruby the first time they met."

Juliet chuckled. "But not you, now you've finally found a man to match you."

"You make Jacob sound like my sparring partner!"

"It's important you have someone who stands up to you as you charge into a situation at full steam, not noticing who you barge into."

"I never charge at anything," I said. "My actions are always well considered."

"And as steadfast as a tank!" Juliet settled a hand on my arm. "It's a compliment. I'm glad you're here to solve this mystery. I would be frantic if you weren't assisting. Freddie does his best to comfort me, but he's not practical."

"Then allow my tank-like ability to grind through the secrets and unearth the truth," I said.

"If Angus wasn't fond of Constance, has anyone else caught his eye?"

Juliet shook her head. "Not that I know of. Why? What have you uncovered? Has he embroiled himself with a servant?"

"It might be nothing."

"Veronica! Don't hide things from me. We used to be the very best of friends when we were younger. We always promised we'd never hide anything from each other."

"There's nothing to hide. I'm pursuing all possibilities to find out what happened in the Thistle Inn."

"Provided I'm not one of those possibilities, you may do as you like." Juliet's eyes narrowed. "I'm not still a suspect, am I?"

"You're a dear friend, but I must keep an open mind."

She huffed an indignant breath. "If you keep talking in that manner, I shall remove you from your bridesmaid duties, too."

Promises, promises.

We returned to the dining room, and I gestured for Ruby to join me.

"Let's get fresh air, shall we? We need to talk, and I don't want to be overheard."

Ruby grimaced as she looked outside, never a fan of exertion in inclement weather. "Could we not take a turn inside the castle? We'll get plenty of exercise if we cover all the floors."

"Now it's light, I want to see if last night's lurker left anything behind and go over everything we have." I herded her towards the door. "Besides, Benji isn't happy being stuck inside. You know he enjoys a walk, whatever the weather."

"Very well." Ruby sighed. "But I'll insist on a hot toddy when we return."

"That sounds like a splendid idea."

Ten minutes later, we were dressed warmly and marching through the pristine snow. The air was crisp and bracing as we walked the castle's perimeter, avoiding the worst of the most recent snowfall.

The crunch of our boots in the snow broke the silence of the harshly beautiful Scottish landscape. Snow lay thick across the moorland, a glittering white carpet stretching to the treeline.

Before heading away from the castle, we'd stopped and inspected the area around the back door and checked the stables but found nothing to suggest there'd been anyone watching the castle last night.

Benji was having a fine old time, weaving in and out of snowdrifts and jumping up to catch snowballs when I tossed them to him.

"I finally spoke to Juliet about what we found in Constance's bedroom," I said.

"Was she surprised?" Ruby asked.

"I kept everything high level, but Juliet had no clue why Constance was so interested in the family history. She also confirmed Constance doesn't come from money."

"All the more reason to think Constance was blackmailing someone," Ruby said.

"Juliet also mentioned Angus and said he's an incorrigible flirt, but he means no harm by it."

"Juliet may have missed something. She has her head full of wedding clouds," Ruby said. "We saw him with Lady Sophia, so we know he can charm anyone."

"It was Lady Sophia who pressed her attention onto Angus. As for his treatment of Constance, we only have Gregor's word for what happened between them," I said.

Ruby hummed to herself. "Could Gregor be deceiving us?"

"Gregor was nervous when we spoke," I said. "But he'll lose everything if it comes to light he's telling lies about the castle's residents."

"Or were his nerves because he was covering his guilt?" Ruby stepped into snow that went up to her knees, causing her to squeak.

"Gregor strikes me as an honest man," I said as I assisted Ruby out of the drift. "But we'll keep him as a suspect since he has no alibi, and he had ample opportunity to commit murder."

"As did Angus," Ruby said. "And he has more of a motive for wanting Constance out of the way."

"Gregor also had concerns about Lord Robert," I said. "He didn't like the way the man watched Constance."

"He is an irascible old fellow," Ruby said. "I didn't mention this yesterday, given how hectic everything was, but he caressed my bottom! I didn't even realise he was there until his hand landed on my derriere."

"What did you do?"

"I froze! If he attempts anything like that again, I'll do what Constance did to Angus and give him a stinging reminder to keep his hands to himself. He may be a lord, but he's no gentleman."

"Indeed. And I'll set Benji on him." I shook my head. "Even though Freddie and Lord Robert were in the room with me, it's possible they paid someone to commit the crime."

"We also have Juliet as a suspect. Motive and an opportunity," Ruby said. "More than one motive, too. And then there's sulky Sophia. They both left the dining room during the time of the murder."

"While we're not short of suspects, we still have the vexing issue of how Constance was killed inside a locked office," I said. "There must be another way in and out of the office that we've yet to find."

Benji froze with one paw in the air, his ears pricked and his hackles lifted. A blur of movement passed behind two nearby trees.

Ruby gasped. "Is that our missing madman?"

I squinted. Whatever was in the treeline was large, dark, and swift.

Benji let out a sharp bark and launched forward, snow spraying behind him.

"Benji, wait!" I shouted, but he was already a streak of determined fur and muscle, bounding towards the trees.

Ruby and I plunged after him, our boots sinking into drifts, breath pluming in the frigid air. Branches clawed at our coats as we pushed into the small copse of firs, the muffled silence broken only by the thud of our footsteps and the rustling ahead.

"There!" Ruby pointed through a gap in the trunks.

A dark figure darted between the trees. They were low to the ground, fast and hunched like an animal, not a madman in a coat. It moved with unsettling speed, scrambling over a fallen log and disappearing behind a rocky outcrop.

Benji didn't hesitate. He bounded up the slope, barking fiercely, his instincts guiding him like a bloodhound on a scent.

Adrenaline pumped through my veins as we scrambled after him.

Ruby was at my side, flushed and panting. "What in heaven's name is that thing? It's too fast to be a person. Is this what Angus and Lady Sophia witnessed last night?"

"Possibly. And in the dark, it would be easy to get confused. Human or not, we need to see where it goes, and make sure Benji comes to no harm."

We crested the rise and skidded to a halt. A narrow path led down to a stream that wound behind the castle, frozen now, the water whispering beneath sheets of ice.

Benji stood at the edge of the bank, growling low, his tail stiff.

The snow was disturbed, and there were prints, deep and oddly shaped, that crisscrossed the bank before vanishing into the undergrowth. Whatever or whoever it was, it had fled across the ice, towards the far edge of the forest.

"These aren't boot prints!" Ruby crouched next to Benji, inspecting the ground.

Benji gave a soft woof then looked back at me, his eyes bright and questioning.

I rested a hand on his head. "Let's get back inside. Whatever that was, it was very real and possibly very dangerous."

"But not a person. Are we dealing with a wild animal?" Ruby grabbed my arm and gasped. "The Terror of Augustine Castle! It chased you when we arrived."

"That's an old tale used to frighten visitors." I scanned the area as we retraced our steps, my senses on high alert as Benji growled.

Ruby looked around, too. "It could have been a large wildcat."

"I'm no expert on big cats, but there may be a creature roaming loose. And those prints are huge."

Ruby's breath plumed out of her in panicked gulps, her head swivelling. "What if it's stalking us right this second?"

"If it is, we'd better pick up the pace. There's nothing to worry about. And there's a hot toddy waiting for you inside." I looked for the enormous shape that had passed between the trees. Everything was silent. There wasn't a whisper of wind, nor a winter songbird making a sound. That was a bad sign. When the wildlife went quiet, you were in trouble.

"Do you see anything?" Ruby whispered.

"No. But let's make haste." I ensured there was no quaver in my voice. "Nobody panic. If there is a creature watching us, a sudden movement could startle it."

"What if it attacks?"

"If anything comes for us, we make as much noise as possible and flap our arms," I said. "Imagine you're facing off with a wild elephant."

"I'd rather not," Ruby said. "Elephants trample."

We continued our retreat through the snow, facing the trees with our backs to the castle. Even Benji walked backwards, picking his paws up high to get through the snow.

"Is that something?" Ruby whispered, her fingers tight on my arm. "A movement to the right. Behind those firs."

I couldn't pick it out. "It's probably the wind."

"What wind? Even nature has frozen in terror at whatever is stalking us!"

"Talk like that induces unnecessary panic," I said. "We're made of sterner stuff than that. You've faced German soldiers and lived to tell the tale."

"How close are we to the castle?" Ruby whispered.

I glanced over my shoulder. Not close enough for my liking. "Almost there. In a few minutes, we'll be inside, laughing at how silly we were to think a Scottish legend grown on village gossip would eat us."

A sudden gust of wind lifted the snow in a swirling sheet, blinding me for a heartbeat. I blinked against the sting, tightening my scarf and pressing forward. Benji stuck close, his ears low, and body alert.

It took another twenty minutes of maintaining our composure while keeping a rigid inspection of the landscape before we reached the safety of the castle wall.

A shadow moved near the entrance we were aiming for. I braced myself but then let out a slow breath as the shape resolved into Angus.

He stepped off the front step, eyes narrowing as he took us in. "What the devil have you two been up to? Playing in the snow? You're covered in it."

"We thought a walk might clear our heads," I said.

"In this weather?" He took Ruby's elbow as she stumbled. "And you look like you've seen a ghost."

"Not a ghost." Ruby brushed snow from her gloves. "Something with paws. Extremely large paws."

Angus glanced at the treeline then back at us. "Come in. There's no use freezing to death chasing shadows."

We followed him inside, snow melting from our boots onto the flagstones, Benji trotting beside us, casting one last look behind him as if he also felt the anxiety caused by such a close call.

Whatever was out there, it would have to wait until we'd solved Constance's murder.

For now, we were safe. But I had a feeling that particular puzzle was far from over.

Chapter 24

"I need an entire bottle of whisky, not just a toddy after that adventure," Ruby declared, cocooned in a thick tartan blanket by the fire.

Benji lay stretched out on the rug, his head on his paws, eyes half-lidded but ears still alert for any danger that may sneak in.

We'd just finished telling Angus and Freddie about our large animal encounter in the snow.

Angus stirred his drink, seated across from us in an armchair that looked too small for his frame. "There have been rumours of big cats in these parts for years, certainly ever since I joined the castle. They're old stories and nothing confirmed, but I've seen a few things that made me pause. Gregor has, too."

"Surely it was a big dog that got loose from the village." Freddie sat near the window, looking out into the snow.

"There were huge tracks and paw prints," I insisted. "Far larger than Benji's."

Freddie gave a short laugh. "A mysterious beast prowling the woods? Such a creature wouldn't survive out there alone."

"We're not inventing this," I said. "Something is out there. Perhaps it's the same thing all of you saw on the night of the murder and then again last night when the lights went out."

"Well, let's suppose there is a rogue animal," Freddie said. "What would it be doing here, at the castle, of all places?"

"Looking for food," Angus said. "If there is a wild animal causing trouble, we need an expert handler. Ah, Gregor, just the man. We need your advice."

I looked at Gregor, who lurked by the door.

Angus stood and strode towards him. "Do you know of any households in the area keeping exotic pets? Big cats, specifically."

He scratched his chin. "There was talk of the Burrell estate having big cats. A tiger, a cheetah, and a panther. They were on the lookout for a lion but weren't having luck finding a breeder or anyone who'd bring one into the country."

"I've heard gossip at the Thistle Inn about the Burrell estate," Angus said. "They're an eccentric family, aren't they?"

"If you don't mind me speaking plainly, people say odd behaviour goes on over there. Eccentric," Gregor said.

Freddie set his cup down with a measured hand. "The Burrells are a complicated family. Old blood. Very formal, ancient bloodlines. A traditional sort. We invited them to the wedding, but they declined."

"You've met them?" I asked.

"A few times at society events. A dinner in Edinburgh, a garden party in Fife. I believe it was a cousin of the baron I spoke with. He struck me as the sort of man who watched the room rather than joined it." Freddie paused. "And there was talk of peculiar habits. A tendency to withdraw due to... episodes."

"Episodes?" Ruby asked.

"Breaks from polite convention," Freddie said carefully. "An acquaintance mentioned a son spent a year in a sanatorium in Switzerland. Exhaustion, they said. But you know how that term is used to mask a myriad of health issues."

"I believe it was the son who collects the animals," Gregor said. "If he's home again, he could have started a new collection."

"How inappropriate," I murmured. "If the roads were clear, I'd head over there and have strong words. Wild beasts shouldn't be in captivity. They rarely thrive. You hear of dreadful cases of animals losing control and attacking because they're confined to a small cage with no stimulation."

"I doubt the young sir would have a care for that," Gregor said. "But if there is a wild animal loose, it must be from that estate."

"No one should go outside until the beast has been shot," Freddie declared.

I stood and glared levelly at him. "No one is shooting anything. That animal didn't ask to be captured and placed in confinement for the entertainment of a gentleman who has less grace than a clipped-winged grouse. It's most likely terrified."

"But it's a danger!" Freddie protested. "You and Ruby could have been killed."

"No shooting!" The gentry's love of shooting anything that moved in the countryside made my stomach churn.

"Why are you all hiding in here?" Lady Sophia arrived, accompanied by Lord Robert and Juliet.

"Veronica and Ruby believe there's a big cat on the prowl," Freddie said. "But we've been forbidden to shoot it."

"Nonsense!" Lord Robert settled into a chair. "On both points. If there is a creature out there terrorising us, then it must be dealt with."

Ignoring his comment, I relayed what had happened outside to a wide-eyed Juliet and a bored-looking Lady Sophia.

"We should set up a trap to contain it," I said.

"You don't even know what it is." Lady Sophia had settled in a seat next to Lord Robert, who was already on the verge of nodding off. "For all you know, it could be diseased."

I headed to the window and joined Freddie. "Could I request Angus and Gregor's help to set traps around the castle to lure the creature to safety?"

"Oh, well, if you must." Freddie looked out of the window, a wistful expression on his face. "But a gun would be far more efficient."

"And an unnecessary use of force." I glared at him until he bobbed his head.

"I'm sure there is something in storage you can use." Freddie looked out over the grounds. "It's a shame the herb garden is hibernating. I spent hours out there last summer learning about the flowers and tinctures you can make with them. Herbs have a calming effect. You could have used some to sedate the beast."

"Who taught you that?" I asked.

"Lord Robert," Freddie said. "He's an encyclopedia of plant knowledge. Fascinating."

I glanced at Lord Robert, who had his head down and was gently snoring. "I didn't realise he had a green finger."

"It's his only hobby," Lady Sophia said. "Well, that and leering at women half his age."

"Hush now," Juliet said. "He's a man from a different era."

"Times change. So should he," Lady Sophia said. "He may act like a doddering old fool, but he's sprightly enough when a pretty face comes into view. Wouldn't you agree, Ruby?"

Ruby lifted her chin but said nothing, although her cheeks burned with indignation that someone had witnessed Lord Robert's inappropriate behaviour towards her.

Lord Robert jerked awake in his seat. "What was that? Did someone say my name?"

"We were discussing our summer tending to the herb garden," Freddie said with fondness.

Lord Robert straightened in his seat. "Herbs have always fascinated my family. A distant relative was believed to be a witch because she brewed tinctures and made pastes for labourers."

"Depending on the time period in question, that would have been a dangerous stereotype to be associated with," I said. "Whispers of being a witch used to be deadly."

"Much like me, she had enormous wealth and a title to protect her," Lord Robert said with an uncalled-for smugness. "Some of her journals survived and are in our private collection here. They make for captivating reading."

"We shall have to take a look," I said. "I have an interest in herbal remedies."

Ruby gave me a curious glance, but I kept my expression neutral. The group continued their conversation about what to do about the big cat, and I excused myself, discreetly gesturing for Ruby to join me.

"What are you up to?" she demanded the second we were out of earshot of everybody.

"We're returning to Constance's bedroom." I was already heading towards the stairs with Benji. "I didn't pay it much attention when we were in the room, but there was an empty teacup with a pungent smell in the bottom."

"But Constance wasn't drugged or poisoned," Ruby said. "We know how she was killed."

"We also know she put up no fight. And I remember how tired she was on the night of the dinner. She yawned repeatedly throughout the first course. What if somebody drugged her?"

"Oh, my! It would have made her easier to kill."

We reached the top of the stairs, and after a quick look around to make sure no one was watching, we slipped into Constance's bedroom.

"She must have dozed off at the desk. It wouldn't have mattered how much noise the killer made because she was sleeping due to whatever was in this." I pointed to the empty cup.

Ruby peered into it and sniffed. "I see what you mean about the smell. There must have been liquid left at the bottom that dried out. It's floral."

"And plenty of herbs, when consumed in a high enough quantity, cause drowsiness," I said.

"We should inspect the pantry," Ruby said. "That's the perfect place to store herbs without causing any suspicion."

"Before we go, I want something. I still can't figure out why Constance researched this castle and the family's history," I said. "I plan to read her entire notebook."

"What about the teacup evidence?" Ruby asked.

"We can't take it, so we need to lock this room. That cup and its contents could be important. Look for a door key. If the killer becomes worried that we're onto them, they could muddy the waters by removing the cup."

"I saw a key on the dressing table," Ruby whispered.

I took the notepad from the travel case and tucked it inside the top of my skirt just as Ruby held up a key with a flourish. We locked the door behind us and hurried downstairs.

There was excited chatter nearby, and we discovered most of the party gathered around the telephone.

"Is it working?" I asked.

"Freddie just checked," Juliet said. "He heard a crackle! He even dialled out to the operator, but the connection didn't hold."

"If it was working, it's not now." Angus was checking the telephone before he placed it back in its cradle. "I propose we all rest and then take lunch together. This is now a waiting game until the authorities arrive. Unless you have any bright ideas, Veronica?"

"I could do with some help to set up traps for the wild animal," I said. "If it returns to the castle, we may be able to capture it."

Angus's brow furrowed. "We'll have something. I'll get Gregor on it."

"Nothing deadly," I instructed. "Place food inside the trap and let it go inside. Do not shoot this creature."

Angus grinned. "We'll get to work."

The party split up, and we headed to an empty reading room, settled in, and sat side by side to read Constance's notes.

"I can see when Constance got excited," Ruby said. "Her handwriting grows untidy."

"Or it's untidy because she was short on time and needed to hurry. She must have done her research when she visited the castle," I said.

"When she should have been wedding planning," Ruby said.

"It makes no sense for Constance to check on deceased ancestors. It's not relevant to Juliet and Freddie's nuptials."

"Perhaps she was looking for a black sheep in the family," Ruby said. "Trying to discredit their name for the blackmail reason we uncovered."

"This is a new name." I pointed to a note. "The lineage dates back to the fifteen hundreds. That's odd. I thought Juliet's family built this castle. That's what she told me. But there's another surname associated with the castle. The Connells."

Ruby peered at the page. "It says here 'lost bet.' Did the Connells lose something to the Augustines?"

I glanced up, taking in the plush surroundings many would desire to own. "What if they lost this castle in a bet?"

"Who would be so foolish as to bet a castle on a game of cards or whatever it was they played?" Ruby exclaimed.

"Perhaps the Connells thought they couldn't lose," I said. "But if someone rigged the game to favour the Augustines..."

"Such a ridiculous bet wouldn't stand up in a court of law."

"Things weren't the same back then," I said. "We need to look into the castle's history. I'm sure Scotland has a magnificent archive, but while we're snowed in, we'll use the resources on hand. Let's visit the library."

Chapter 25

"What shall we say if anyone finds us in here?" Ruby asked as we slipped into the magnificent library, all polished dark wood with luxurious gold fabric wallpaper and floor-to-ceiling book stacks.

"We're looking at the journals Lord Robert's witch ancestor left behind," I said. "Claim you have an interest in gardening."

Ruby chortled. "I don't even have a potted plant. I always forget to water the poor things, and they shrivel and the leaves drop off."

"Let's hope you take better care of Grace."

"Veronica! Never compare my daughter to a potted plant." Ruby laughed. "Although if plants fretted as much as she did when she needed feeding, I'd always remember to water them."

"Grace does make that rather odd noise when it's time to feed."

"Her adorable gurgle, you mean?"

"I was referring to the screaming. You start on one end, and I'll start over here," I said. "Look for books about the castle or the family."

"If Constance figured out the family obtained this castle through dubious means, did she use it for her own gain?" Ruby asked.

"The money in her possession suggests blackmail," I said. "If Constance disclosed this information, it would ruin the Augustine name."

"Constance approached Juliet and demanded money to ensure her silence?"

"It may not have been Juliet." I ran my fingers along the spines of the beautiful leather-bound books. "Lady Sophia and Lord Robert are a part of this family, too."

"Well, that's jolly unhelpful. We have an additional motive, but it doesn't narrow the suspects. Here! This is the section on local history."

"Gather everything. It could all be valuable."

The next hour passed in silence as we read the six books about the castle and the Augustine family, each taking three books and the notebook from Constance's belongings for comparison.

A noise outside caught my attention, and I spotted Angus and Gregor hauling a large cage through the grounds. I was delighted to see they carried no guns.

I grew frustrated as another hour passed and I'd unearthed nothing helpful, though I'd been fascinated by a castle schematic showing the extensive tunnel network. The lengths members of the household used to go to avoid tradesmen and staff were extensive.

Ruby was in the same predicament. Her stomach grumbled, and mine soon joined in, making Benji jerk awake and stare at me, his head cocked.

I chuckled at his response. "It will soon be time to eat."

"This could be something." Ruby handed me a book. "It mentions a rivalry between the Connells and the Augustine family. They fought on opposing sides in an old war. The families have held a grudge ever since, often disputing land boundaries."

I took the book and skimmed the passage. "It makes no mention of the Connells losing this castle to anyone."

"Perhaps it's not recorded in Juliet's family history," Ruby said. "They'd want to keep it quiet to avoid anyone protesting and putting ownership at risk."

"Which is what Constance did when she discovered the truth," I murmured.

"She demanded money to remain silent, but in doing so, she sealed her fate," Ruby said. "A family member wasn't willing to trust her or was worried she'd return and make additional demands."

"The Augustine family is ridiculously wealthy. So is Freddie's family. Join those fortunes, and you'd have a continuous tap of money to manipulate. Constance would have known this information."

Ruby sat back in her seat. "But how are we to figure out which family member silenced Constance for good?"

"That lunch hit the spot." Freddie patted his stomach. "I'd suggest a walk, but I fear there may be more big cats on the loose and they'll gobble us up."

We'd all gathered for a spot of lunch, forcing a break from our studies into the Augustine family history.

"It's sensible to stay inside until the grounds are safe," I said. "If one cat escaped, there could be more. And we only have so many cages."

"That would explain the multiple sightings," Angus said. "I've been blaming them on too much whisky downed by Thistle Inn patrons, but it seems we have a real problem."

Lady Sophia tutted. "Not only am I trapped inside by this snow, but now hungry wild animals want to devour me."

"They won't be interested in you," Juliet said. "There's barely any meat on your bones."

"If it categorises its meals in that manner, you should be careful. Your wedding diet has failed. It must be all the golden syrup you've been sneaking off to eat."

Juliet scowled at her. "Make up your mind. Not so long ago, you said I was so thin I looked consumptive."

"I said you looked pale, not thin."

Juliet huffed an objection, but Angus interrupted the squabble, smiling broadly as he stood from his seat. "Would anyone like apple crumble? I'm no gourmet chef, but my granny taught me this recipe, and I've made a huge batch."

Juliet clapped her hands together. "How delightful. Yes, please."

Everyone else nodded, apart from Lady Sophia, who wrinkled her nose.

"I'll be right back," Angus said.

True to his word, Angus bounded back in, holding a steaming dish of crumble, and Ruby assisted him with passing out bowls.

"Oh, my! That smells delicious." Juliet helped herself to a generous portion under Lady Sophia's withering gaze.

"None for me," Lady Sophia said when Angus offered her the dessert.

"I shouldn't, but I adore crumble," Juliet said, her spoon already full. "I'll have to wait at least an hour before I do my afternoon stretches after this feast."

"You have an exercise routine?" I asked.

"I've kept up my ballet education," Juliet said. "It keeps me supple. I'm not one for romping in the fields and getting dirty, but I enjoy regular exercise."

I nodded, recalling the hours of practice Juliet undertook. She'd attempted to get me interested in ballet, but I couldn't abide the clothing and shoes. I was very much a romper in the fields.

"I don't know why you bother. You're too old and plump to be a ballerina," Lady Sophia said.

"I could never get the hang of it," Ruby said. "My parents forced me to learn, but I only performed once. After that disaster, when I pirouetted and landed in some poor man's lap, the teacher advised me to try something more sedentary."

"What did you select?" Freddie asked.

"I'm an expert rider. You need outstanding balance for that."

"Or the ability to hold tight and dig in your heels." Lady Sophia pushed her chair away from the table. "Unless anyone else is murdered, I'm not to be disturbed." She left the room.

"Sophia wasn't always this sour," Juliet said with a sigh. "But as she gets older, she gets meaner."

"Perhaps her sharpness is because of the divorce," Ruby suggested. "Or she could be jealous of your happiness. Her heart's been broken while yours glows with joy."

Juliet scooped up more apple crumble. "I'm sure you're right. But she's been an absolute horror recently."

"Is her husband not holding up his end of the divorce?" I asked.

"It's possible he's being stingy with her. Sophia mentioned some unwise investments during the war, which resulted in them losing a sizeable sum of money." Juliet slapped a hand over her mouth then lowered it. "Forget I mentioned that. She'd tear my hair out if she thought I was gossiping about her financial distress."

"A broken heart and an empty purse would make me miserable, too," Ruby said. "Now, let's polish off this delicious crumble, shall we? We can be plump former ballerinas together."

Fifteen minutes later, we left the remaining guests with their coffee and snuck into the castle's kitchen.

We hurried directly to a huge walk-in pantry. It was a vast space, the walls lined with deep shelves, and we took a moment to locate the herbs and spices.

"I'm no expert," Ruby said after a moment of searching, "but chamomile is soothing."

"We also have dried lavender and apple here," I said. "In the right combination, it would make Constance so tired she couldn't fight back. Add in some medicine—"

"What medicine?"

"Lord Robert took a pill when we were at dinner on the night of Constance's murder. I'm uncertain what condition it treats, but he said they make him tired."

"They won't be for his lacklustre libido," Ruby said.

"Indeed, not. He nods off frequently. That could be a side effect of the medication. If one of his pills was slipped into Constance's food or drink, it would have added to her tiredness."

"Does that mean we must search his luggage to find out what he takes?"

"Goodness! What are you both doing in here?" Juliet appeared in the pantry doorway, mild surprise on her face.

"We were considering baking to pass the time," I lied smoothly. "Are you here for more pickles and syrup?"

"I've gone off syrup." Juliet eyed me with suspicion. "What are you really doing here? Veronica, I know very well you have no aptitude for the kitchen. I recall the failed sponge cakes you baked at Sunday school. No one ever wanted to try anything you whipped up. Even the priest lied to avoid trying your baking disasters. And those rock cakes you baked one day almost chipped a tooth."

"The very scandal." Ruby laughed. "You made a man of the cloth tell a falsehood to avoid your food."

"Perhaps I've changed," I said, feeling my cheeks heat.

"Not likely." Juliet arched an eyebrow. "Are you looking for clues? The escaped animal has distracted all of us, but your mind is still churning over the evidence."

I glanced at Ruby. I'd known Juliet since we were children. Perhaps letting slip information might help. Or get a confession. "I have a theory about what happened to Constance."

"Something other than her being stabbed?" Juliet asked.

"I think someone drugged her to make her pliable."

"Drugged! Gosh. That's shocking. But we don't have drugs in the kitchen," Juliet said.

"Herbs can be powerful. Add in a sedative and Constance would have been vulnerable," I said.

Juliet took a few seconds to process. "I'm confused. We all saw a dagger sticking out of Constance's back. Isn't that what killed her?"

"But she didn't fight back," I said. "Wouldn't you?"

"Not if my attacker surprised me." Juliet's hand fluttered in the air. "Oh, dear. What a terrible thought! I need a biscuit." She popped the lid off a tin and helped herself to several digestive biscuits before offering them round.

"Does Lord Robert use medication to calm his nerves?" I asked.

Juliet's forehead wrinkled. "He takes pills for his legs. They cause him pain. Would that be what you're looking for?"

"It might. Pain medication can often make one tired."

"Who would have taken his pills, though?"

"That's what we need to find out," I said. "Did you need something from the pantry?"

"I overdid the apple crumble." Juliet looked at the biscuits and blushed. "I was looking for something to settle my stomach."

"There's dried peppermint," Ruby said. "I find that useful when I've had one too many slices of cake."

Juliet hesitated. "No. I'm feeling better now. Although a lie-down is in order."

"No stretching?" I asked.

"Later. It's always annoying when Sophia is right, but I have no control over my appetite because of, well, you know what. Let me know what you find out, and I'll have words with whoever took medicine from my uncle." Juliet left us to continue searching through the herbs.

I watched her go. Had Juliet followed us to see if we'd discovered her herbal secret, or was the visit a coincidence?

"I've lost count of the outfits Juliet has with her," Ruby said as she turned back to the shelves. "She must have several cupboards full of clothing stored here."

"I expect so," I said.

"She even changed outfits between courses the night we dined together," Ruby said. "She came down in such a stunning red dress, but when she joined us in the Thistle Inn, she wore a different red dress. Still beautiful, but I thought it was excessive to change between courses."

I turned to Ruby, my gaze widening. "You're right! You're always more observant of fashion than me."

Ruby ran a critical eye over my clothing. "I have no choice. You'd wear your mother's hand-me-downs if I let you get away with it."

"There's nothing wrong with make do and mend." I closed my eyes as I recalled what Juliet wore on the night of Constance's murder.

"There is when there's too much tweed involved," Ruby said.

I abandoned the search in the pantry. "Come with me."

"Where are we going now? Don't we have herbs to check?"

"We must find the dress Juliet wore on the night of the dinner. And then we need to sneak into the office to check something."

"Something that will reveal who the killer is?" Ruby hurried along with me.

"Yes! Our studies have borne fruit." I drew in a breath. "Thanks to you, I believe I know who killed Constance."

Chapter 26

"I have excellent news!" Freddie strode into the parlour we'd all gathered in before our evening meal. "The telephone is working, and the police are on their way."

"That's splendid," Juliet said. "This business will soon be over, and then we can focus on our happy day. Once Constance's body has been removed, I'll feel so much better about getting married."

Angus dashed in with Gregor behind him. "My apologies for interrupting, but we've seen something outside."

I was about to present the evidence to the waiting party as to who killed Constance, but that would have to wait. "Is it a cat?"

"Gregor got the best look." Angus nudged Gregor forward.

"I... I can't be certain because it's so dark, but something took food from a cage." Gregor clutched his cap in his hand. "I crept to the next cage and startled something away."

My gaze shot to the window. "How many cages did you set out?"

"Four. One at each corner of the castle," Gregor said.

"I'll get the guns from the cupboard." Lord Robert hauled himself to his feet. "Gentlemen, you're with me."

"You'll do no such thing," I snapped.

"Young lady, I've had enough of you telling people what to do." Lord Robert wheeled on me with surprising speed for a man of his age. "This is the family estate, and if there is a wild creature causing a nuisance, it's my right to shoot it. And I'll shoot you if you get in my way."

"Shoot me, and you'll answer to the law," I said coldly. "And I'm quite certain you wouldn't last long in a prison cell. There are no whisky decanters or cigars in there to pass the time, and certainly no ladies for you to bother with your unwanted comments."

Lord Robert flushed an unpleasant shade. "Come, Gregor. And you too, Angus. Let's sort this once and for all."

Freddie stepped forward. "No one is going anywhere until we have a sensible plan."

Lord Robert grumbled, eyes smouldering. "I'll remind you that you're not yet a part of this family. When you are, then you can have a say in matters that concern this castle."

Freddie's chin wobbled, but he didn't argue back.

Angus gave me an apologetic glance. "Stay inside, everyone, until this matter is finished."

I followed them to the door with Ruby and Benji, and once armed with shotguns, the three men strode out into the snow, and the door shut with a heavy thud.

"We're not staying inside, are we?" Ruby whispered to me.

"Not a chance," I murmured. "Get your coat."

Moments later, we slipped outside. The cold hit like a slap, sharp and bracing. Benji trotted at our heels, his paws silent on the snow. Ahead, the men's lanterns bobbed in the dark.

We veered off the main path and cut across to the far side of the castle. Our breaths came in little white bursts as we hurried along.

"There's a cage," Ruby whispered, pointing ahead of us.

A cage loomed ahead near the orchard wall. Light from inside the castle revealed something had been captured. It was a dark mass hunched low, tail lashing against the bars. The smell was sharp and musky.

"We got here in time," I murmured. "Now we just need to bash sense into Lord Robert to stop him from pulling the trigger."

The shape inside the cage shifted, and gleaming eyes flashed. Then, with a sudden metallic shriek, the door swung wide and the creature burst out. It landed in the snow and wheeled to face us.

Ruby gripped my sleeve, while Benji barked furiously.

It was a huge black cat! The beast crouched, its muscles rippling, and its breath pluming in the freezing air. For a heartbeat, none of us moved.

The creature let out a low, guttural sound and crouched.

"Don't move," I hissed. "Maybe it's used to people and won't see us as a threat."

The cat sprang.

We turned and ran. Snow sprayed up with each frantic step as we bolted.

"Benji! With us!" I yelled. My dog was fearlessly loyal and would put himself in harm's way if he thought it would protect me or Ruby.

The deep snow meant there was no formal path to follow, and we kept landing in drifts up to our thighs, slowing our progress. Fortunately, the cat also struggled in the snow, but it was still coming as it snarled and panted.

Ruby gasped, her feet sliding out from underneath her, and she landed with a grunt on her back, losing her grip on my arm.

I skidded to a halt. I wasn't leaving my best friend. I turned, planting myself firmly in front of her. I inhaled sharply and raised my arms above my head to look as intimidating as possible.

When the panic stopped rattling my brain, I relaxed a fraction. Speed limping towards us was a clearly undernourished wild cat with dark fur. And from the way it staggered and struggled to breathe, it appeared to be on its last legs.

It paused when it saw me watching but made no move to attack.

I lowered my arms. "Well, you're not so terrifying, are you?"

Benji was by my side, growling at the cat, which snarled back with twice the viciousness, making the hairs on my arms lift.

Slowly, I rested my hand on Benji's head, ensuring he settled and made no heroic moves. I made soothing, soft sounds to settle Benji and the large cat.

The creature stopped five feet away from me and stared.

"Why isn't it eating us?" Ruby whispered, still in the snow.

"I'm uncertain, but I don't think this creature is a threat. It looks half-starved and injured."

Ruby hauled herself out of the snow, causing the cat to growl. She froze, still on her hands and knees. "What should I do?"

"Stand slowly. Make no sudden movements. I have an idea."

"Any idea that gets us out of this predicament works for me." Ruby took a moment to stand. Snow covered her, and her teeth chattered.

I hunted through my coat pockets and pulled out a handful of meaty chews Benji enjoyed. I tossed one at the big cat.

It snarled, but then its nostrils quivered. A second later, it darted forward, grabbed the food, and gulped it down without even chewing.

"Oh, it does look bedraggled," Ruby whispered. "Why let such a magnificent creature get so thin?"

"I imagine it costs a pretty penny to induce a veterinarian to treat such an animal," I muttered. "And it may not be in the country legally, so if it is unwell, there'd be nowhere to take it."

"If it's not completely wild, does that mean it doesn't want to eat us?"

"It would chew on us if it had the opportunity," I said, "but this creature has clearly been around humans. It may even have chased us for help. Let's lead it back to the castle. There are stables we can use to keep it in."

"Won't it escape?"

"It must be as terrified as we are," I said. "If it's used to a life of luxury with food on tap and suddenly found itself abandoned and sick in a freezing Scottish winter, it'll be panicked. If we offer shelter, food, water, and a safe place to sleep, the creature will be grateful."

"I hope you've got enough treats to keep its gratitude intact," Ruby said.

"Back slowly towards the castle with Benji and keep an eye out for our gun toting friends," I said. "I'll follow and keep the cat occupied with the treats."

With a plan in hand, we edged around the side of the castle and towards the stables. There were no horses in residence, so Ruby found the first available stable and opened the door.

"It's clean, and there's plenty of straw in here," she said.

"Find a water container." I kept my attention on the big cat. "And make sure the locks are sturdy in case it tries to break out."

After a few minutes of scrambling around and tossing treats, everything was ready.

I studied the cat as we led it into the sanctuary of the castle walls. It was a pitiful sight. Patches of dark fur were missing, and one paw was barely usable as it limped along.

"You poor creature," I murmured.

It disgusted me when people didn't take proper care of their animals. When you invited an animal into your family, it became a part of that family. It wasn't an object to show off, mistreat, or toss aside when you grew bored. Would you do that to your elderly grandmother? Sadly, some people would.

I backed past the open stable door, giving the big cat room. Then I tossed the final few treats inside.

The creature made no protest and limped into the stable, not even reacting when we shut the door and bolted it.

I breathed a sigh of relief just as I saw Angus approaching with his gun. There would be no shooting tonight or any night. Now that problem was solved, all we needed to do was uncover Constance's killer, and I'd finally get a good night's rest.

Chapter 27

"The Terror of Augustine Castle really was an escaped big cat." Freddie shook his head in stunned disbelief as he warmed himself by the fire. "How old is this creature? People have been telling tales about it for decades."

I'd just returned to the drawing room with Ruby and Benji after changing out of wet clothing and then conducting a swift search for the final clue to catch our killer.

"It may not be the first to escape from the Burrells' private collection," I said. "From its bedraggled appearance, I would say it's been on its own for some time. I could see rib bones, and it consumed Benji's treats in seconds."

"I still think we should have shot it." Lord Robert was back by the fire too, not looking happy at being bested by two women and a dog.

"Uncle Robert! The poor creature can't hurt us now," Juliet said. "We're safe, and so is the cat. I'm jolly glad Veronica caught it."

"The capture was all thanks to Angus and Gregor for setting the cages to lure in the creature." I said.

"Not as well as we should have." Angus glanced at Gregor, who stood close to the wall. "I thought those springs would hold. You could have been killed."

"Well, we weren't. And everything has worked out for the best," I said brightly.

"Imagine what would have happened if the rest of our guests had reached the castle." Juliet shuddered. "The creature would have picked them off one by one."

"Not me." Lady Sophia was looking out the window, her back to us. "Whoever is the slowest runner would be that mangy old creature's next meal."

"Don't be so unpleasant," Juliet said. She turned her attention back to me and Ruby. "You must have been terrified when it chased you."

"There were a few seconds when I thought my heart had stopped," Ruby said. "But Veronica saved the day."

"There was nothing to fear. When I took a second to study the creature, I realised it wasn't chasing us to eat us. It wanted human company and help."

"Poppycock! These wild creatures aren't that intelligent," Lord Robert said.

"This one is. And I'd wager it's more domestic than wild," I said.

Angus narrowed his eyes. "If it's not wild, why did it chase you and Benji when you first arrived? I reckon that was the same creature that set its sights on you."

"Perhaps it was hunting Benji," I conceded. "To a big cat, Benji would look like a meal."

"I'm glad it failed," Juliet said. "Benji's a sweetheart."

Benji, who was drying out in front of the fire as well, wagged his tail as he heard his name, happy to agree he'd make a terrible meal for a big cat.

"What should we do with it?" Juliet asked.

"Shoot it," Lord Robert said.

"I'll shoot him if he doesn't pipe down," Ruby whispered to me.

"It can stay where it is for now," I said. "But I would like to look at its injuries. It has a damaged paw. If infection sets in, it may lose its leg."

"It's too risky to examine a wild animal," Angus said. "Even if the cat is used to humans, it won't know you. And as you said, it's terrified. Frightened animals are dangerous."

I didn't want to risk the creature's life, but I also didn't want to lose a hand examining its injury. "I'll take another look, and if the cat shows no sign of fever, we'll organise treatment in the morning. For now, we keep it warm, watered, and well-fed."

Angus nodded his approval

"Now, I'm glad you're all here," I said. "Our new arrival quite distracted me, but I need to let you know that we've uncovered what happened to Constance."

There were several surprised noises, and the group exchanged glances.

"And since we've discounted the deranged stranger on the loose theory," Ruby said, "the killer must be in this very room."

That comment garnered more noises of surprise.

"Do you know who murdered Constance?" Freddie asked in a hushed tone.

"Yes. And we have the evidence to prove it." I looked at Ruby, and she nodded at me.

Our search in the Thistle Inn office and a check of a certain clothing item had given me a result that didn't thrill me, but the evidence was never wrong, so it was time to unveil the truth.

"Don't keep us in suspense," Angus said.

Lady Sophia had turned from the window, a glint of sharp interest in her eyes.

"When Constance's body was discovered in the Thistle Inn office, I ruled out Freddie and Lord Robert as possible killers, since the three of us were at the table at the time of the murder," I said.

"That's right. We're innocent," Freddie said.

"Innocent of plunging the dagger into Constance's back, but one of you is an accessory to this dreadful crime," I said.

Freddie turned confused eyes to Juliet and Lord Robert.

"Lord Robert. Freddie revealed to me your interest in herbs," I said. "You must know about their powerful properties."

"I can't say I do. I enjoy growing them, but that is all." Lord Robert regarded me with a flat stare of disbelief that I dared to address him.

Freddie startled. "You're always telling me about herbs' properties when we prune them."

Lord Robert adjusted his position in the chair by the fire. "I can't recall such conversations, but I'm old. I barely remember one week from the next."

"You used herbs and the medication you take to subdue Constance," I said. "I noticed how tired she was throughout our first course when we dined together."

"Why would I want a young lady subdued?" Lord Robert was now fully alert, gripping the arms of his chair.

"Because this murder was a family affair," I said. "At first, I suspected Angus was involved. He was romantically interested in Constance, and she rejected his advances. A man's ego makes him do unpleasant things when he's slighted."

"I have great respect for women." Angus carefully set down his glass. "And I supported you when you wanted to investigate this murder. Not everyone in this castle was so obliging."

"And I appreciated that," I said. "You and Gregor have helped us to eliminate suspects. Neither of you had solid alibis, but I found no motive for Gregor, and as we delved deeper into the clues, it became clear that the killer was a part of this family."

"You claim this is a family affair." Lady Sophia glared at me, no longer relaxed. "But it makes more sense for a man to commit such a vicious crime."

"And one man was involved," I said. "Lord Robert ensured Constance was compliant, so she would be easy to murder."

"Not by my hand!" Lady Sophia said.

"Veronica! What are you saying?" Juliet gasped. "If Angus and Gregor are innocent, and Uncle Robert drugged Constance, which I don't believe he would, that only leaves me or Sophia, and neither of us did it!"

"The evidence says otherwise," I said, squashing the twist of regret in my gut.

"What evidence?" Lady Sophia snapped. "You keep mentioning evidence, but you present nothing. This is a bluff, hoping someone will be woolly-headed enough to confess."

"Then allow me to be clear," I said. "Constance's notebook. A carelessly left teacup. A large amount of money. A soiled dress. And the original castle plans. They provided everything we needed to solve this crime."

The group sat in silence as they waited for me to continue, the tension in the air sending a shiver down my spine.

"Who does all that lead to?" Angus asked.

"Before I get to that, I searched Constance's room with Ruby and Benji," I said. "We found a teacup containing the remnants of an herbal tea. When we compared the scents with herbs in the pantry, we discovered the tea would have had a sedative effect. On their own, they wouldn't have knocked Constance out, but add in Lord Robert's medication, crushed into the tea, and Constance would have felt excessively weary."

"That proves nothing," Lady Sophia said. "She could have made that tea herself. Perhaps all of Juliet's bothersome demands prevented her from sleeping."

"On its own, that evidence isn't enough to secure a conviction," I agreed. "But Constance's notebook was a fascinating read. When she visited the castle to prepare Juliet and Freddie's wedding, she wasn't just working. She was researching the castle's history. What do you think she discovered?"

"I don't have the faintest idea. History is an excessively dull topic." Lady Sophia looked away, but not before I saw her jaw clench.

"Constance didn't think so. She discovered the original castle owners, the Connells, lost their home in a bet. A bet placed by your family. Juliet, you told me your family built this castle, but that's not true, is it?" I asked.

"How ... how would I know?" Juliet said.

"Perhaps you didn't realise how your family came into possession of this castle," I continued, "but when Constance found out, she confronted you. Or perhaps it was Lady Sophia. Which of you did she think would be the most receptive to a touch of blackmail?"

"Blackmail! It certainly wasn't me. I barely spoke to the woman," Lady Sophia said.

"Constance threatened to expose the truth," I said. "If a modern court of law determined this castle was gained through illicit means, they might return it to the original family. There would be no perfect castle wedding if you didn't have a castle."

"Which is why one of you paid for Constance's silence," Ruby said.

I nodded. "And the police will check if either of you made a significant transfer of funds."

"They won't find any payments from me," Juliet said. "This is all nonsense."

Lady Sophia huffed out a small breath of annoyance. "I'm allowed to do what I like with my money."

"And if you had money, that wouldn't be a problem," I said. "But Constance wasn't content with a single payment, was she? She demanded more. And that left you in a quandary. You'd run out of funds if you kept buying her silence."

Lady Sophia lifted her chin. "It may have escaped your middle-class attention, but I have extensive wealth."

"Not anymore," I said. "Juliet kindly made us aware of your financial struggles."

Lady Sophia shot daggers at Juliet. "Struggles. I'm not in the poorhouse!"

"But you didn't have enough money to guarantee Constance's silence. And I'm certain you begrudged every penny you gave her," I said. "The only way to ensure her silence forever was to kill her."

"It wasn't me!" Lady Sophia protested. "Maybe I gave the foolish woman a few pounds to keep her deceitful tongue from wagging, but that was all I did. I... I am fond of Augustine Castle, despite its drafts and outrageous heating bills. I didn't wish for it to be taken. Not in such a deceitful manner. It was wrong."

"I agree you didn't touch the dirk that killed Constance. But you came up with the plan together," I said. "All three of you. You couldn't risk losing this castle and having your family name tarnished. When the blackmail demands became too much, you helped each other. Lord Robert drugged Constance. And Juliet murdered her."

"Impossible!" Juliet's composure slipped, and panic flared in her eyes. "Veronica, we're friends. You know I'm not capable of committing such an awful act."

"Why did you change your dress between dinner courses?" I asked.

"I ... I didn't do that."

"I remember you wore a different dress," Ruby said. "Two red dresses on that night."

"Oh! Well, I didn't feel pretty in the first dress," Juliet said. "There's no crime in changing your clothes."

"We found the first dress you wore," I said. "You hadn't hidden it well enough at the back of your wardrobe. It was torn and covered in soot. Can you tell us why that would be?"

Juliet paled. "You had no right to go through my things. You have betrayed our friendship."

"And you had no right to plunge a dagger into Constance's back," I said. "You know every inch of this castle since you spent summers here as a child, playing with friends, chasing each other, enjoying a game of hide and seek. You knew about the tunnels and which rooms they led to."

"I'm sorry for interrupting, but we inspected those tunnels," Angus said. "We found no signs that anyone had used them."

"We missed a route," I said. "I checked the original castle drawings and discovered a passageway built inside the main chimney stacks. Chimney sweeps used them to avoid covering the rooms in soot. They would climb down the passage as they cleaned."

"I'm at a loss to see how this is relevant," Freddie said.

"Juliet revealed she kept up with her ballet practice. Ballerinas are excessively strong, so she has ample strength to climb or descend a brick passage," I said. "Juliet excused herself during dinner, went to the first floor, climbed down the chimney stack, and entered the office."

"Well, I'll be blowed," Gregor murmured, who'd been listening to every word with a silent intensity.

"My sweet, you ... you didn't do this, did you?" Freddie shook as he slid away from Juliet.

Juliet gulped and looked at Lady Sophia and Lord Robert. Neither met her gaze. Her panic turned to anger.

"Constance planned on making her fortune off you," I said. "Not through the wedding, but through blackmail. This family is traditional and well-respected. You had to prevent a scandal."

"I told them this plan would fail," Lady Sophia muttered. "But you can't reason with the foolish."

"Be quiet!" Juliet hissed.

"Your friend isn't stupid," Lady Sophia continued. "Nosy, irritating, and too curious for her own good, but she won't give up. And when the police contact my bank, they'll learn the truth about my... donations. I refuse to be charged with the murder you committed."

A shocked silence filled the room.

Juliet leapt from her seat. "You told me the passage would be easy to climb down. I almost broke my neck doing your dirty work! Literal dirty work, since the footholds were filthy and broken. You said everything had been cleaned, and it would take a minute to descend."

"My dirty work?" Lady Sophia glowered at Juliet. "You made your choices. I had nothing to do with that."

Juliet's cheeks flamed scarlet. "This is our family's castle. I had every right to defend it!"

"Oh, my sweet. Why didn't you come to me? I could have helped if money was an issue," Freddie said.

Juliet pushed him. "You nincompoop! Do you have any idea how expensive castles are to maintain? I'll inherit this pile, and we can't afford an expensive legal scandal or to have the family name raked through the muck. That's what Constance threatened to do."

Freddie puffed out his chest, disappointment in his eyes. "I may not own a castle, but I understand how these things work. Murder is never the answer."

"You're as naïve as you are weak-chinned," Lady Sophia scoffed. "And since it escaped your notice, Juliet doesn't love you. She wants your money to keep the castle going. It wasn't only my husband who invested foolishly during the war."

"You've ruined everything! I hate you all." Juliet dashed to the door, pulled it open, and fled along the hallway.

"Benji. Fetch!" I ordered.

I was certain Juliet wouldn't flee far, but with such heightened emotions, I couldn't risk her doing something foolish to escape punishment.

Benji raced after Juliet, and we hurried after them as a one.

Juliet tugged open the door to the stable yard, with Benji still in pursuit. She screamed and staggered back. The big cat stood in the yard, snarling at her.

Benji lunged, tackling Juliet to the floor, while I swiftly shut the door to ensure the cat didn't decide that coming inside to warm its paws was a good idea.

Angus peered out the window. "Oh! There's a stroke of luck. Here comes the cavalry. I'd better ensure they know we have an unfriendly guest on the loose. Gregor, you're with me."

I glanced outside to see two police cars and a large, dark van pull up. "Better late than never."

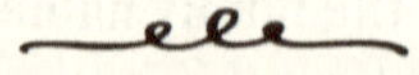

The castle was finally quiet after hours of extensive questioning and the presentation of evidence. Police officers moved in and out of the grand entrance through the snow, escorting Juliet, Lady Sophia, and Lord Robert to waiting cars. They wore expressions ranging from furious to utterly defeated as they accepted their fate.

Ruby, Benji, Angus, Gregor, and I watched in the darkness as justice was carried out. Freddie stood apart from us, close to the cars, his hands in his pockets. He looked ... well, not heartbroken, but certainly glum.

"That's one way to end this wedding," Angus said. "They got so close to saying 'I do'. Did Juliet really only want to marry Sir Frederick for the money?"

"There must have been some affection," Ruby said. "A baby on the way is evidence they were close."

"A baby!" Angus's mouth dropped open.

"Oops! I shouldn't have said that." Ruby lifted one shoulder. "But all truths in this matter need to be told."

"A baby will ensure Juliet receives an income from Freddie's family," I said. "Assuming the judge lets her keep the child."

"It won't be the first time an innocent has been used in such a manner," Ruby said. "And they'll need it if the family finances are so badly stretched."

"Perhaps this extravagant wedding pushed things over the edge. Juliet's family paid for every one of her demands," I said. "And they were quite some demands."

The van door shut, and an officer raised a hand to let us know they were leaving.

"Gregor, is there any news from the veterinarian?" I asked.

"Provided he can get through the snow, he'll be here at dawn," he said.

"I'll get the tractor out first thing and help with the clearing," Angus said.

"Excellent." Although I had contacts in animal rescue, they didn't stretch to wild animal vets. Fortunately, the wonderful people at the dogs' home I volunteered at raced into action and found someone local to assist, and I was already reaching out to find somewhere suitable for the cat to spend the rest of its days free from fear and with all the food it desired.

"The creature will be no bother now it's back in the stable," Gregor said.

"And it only took a few venison cuts to convince it back inside," Angus said with a rueful smile. "I checked the bolts, and one was rusty, so it must have knocked the door loose."

"I'm glad it did," I said. "Otherwise, Juliet would have fled into the Scottish wilds."

"Nonsense! Benji would never have allowed that." Ruby crouched and fussed over a contented Benji.

Freddie slouched over to join us. After a long, drawn-out sigh, he turned to Ruby. "Well, that was a dreadful shame. A wedding cancelled, and I find myself tragically single, despite being an eligible bachelor. Would you care to—"

"No," Ruby said before he could finish.

Freddie blinked. "I haven't even made my offer."

"And yet, I know what it would be." Ruby patted his arm. "I stand by my answer."

Angus coughed, clearly holding back a laugh, and even the usually timid Gregor looked amused.

"Well," Freddie sniffed. "I'm considered quite a catch, you know."

"I'm sure you are," Ruby said kindly.

Freddie harrumphed. "I have an estate in Hampshire."

"Country life isn't for me. I'm a city girl. London is my home."

"I have a flat in Mayfair. Would that do?"

"For your perfect lady, I'm sure it would." Ruby's eyes twinkled with fond amusement. "That lady isn't me. And you wouldn't want a teary-eyed war widow with a young child, would you?"

"Ah! Perhaps not. I see your point. Well made. You understand, I had to ask." Freddie glanced at me, but a warning growl from Benji convinced him not to risk making the same foolish proposition. "Until I find my perfect lady, I shall have to console myself with wedding champagne. We have twenty crates to make our way through."

"And cake!" Ruby said. "All five tiers going to waste would be a tragedy. And one we can prevent. Veronica and I had hoped for a small holiday after the wedding until murder tattered that plan."

"We can't have you ladies missing your holiday." Angus flashed a sturdy knee from beneath his kilt. "May I propose, with your permission, Sir Frederick, that we make the best of this situation and enjoy some cake and champagne?"

Everyone agreed that was an excellent idea, including Benji, who bounced around the small group as if someone had just suggested a five-mile hike.

It wasn't the happy ending anyone had planned. The wedding was ruined, reputations shattered, and lives had been upended *and* ended. But this was the ending that was deserved. Justice had been served. And that was more important than a perfect wedding.

I patted Benji. "After cake and champagne, let's plan how we'll convince Ruby and Grace that a walking holiday in the Scottish Highlands will be a splendid affair."

"I heard that!" Ruby said. "You promised me lavish dinners and fine castles, not stomping about in the snow and muck. And I've quite gone off the great outdoors since a big cat almost ate me."

"You've never liked the great outdoors." I laughed as I chivvied my friend along and we turned to the grand castle, beautiful under its blanket of snow. Augustine Castle was safe, and the Thistle Inn patrons would have a thrilling tale to mull over when the doors reopened.

Ruby caught hold of my elbow. "Don't you think Grace would make an adorable flower girl?"

"She can't even walk," I said. "Besides, who is getting married? Please don't tell me you've accepted another inappropriate proposal?"

"Pish! Not me. But I have been in conversation with Jacob—"

"That's quite enough gossip! Jacob is happy just as we are." I guided Ruby into the castle.

"I'm just suggesting, when the time is right, how adorable Grace would be in a gorgeous frock with flowers in her hair. Oh! Look at that." She let go of my arm and dashed ahead just as Angus wheeled the wedding cake out of the kitchen.

I'd have to squash this commentary as quickly as possible. I was content. Jacob was content, and life was complicated enough without adding a wedding. I'd just witnessed the tragic outcome of mingling complex families.

The telephone rang, and everybody cheered.

Since Angus was dealing with the cake, and Gregor and Freddie had gone to the cellar to collect champagne, Ruby answered. After a second, she turned to me, a sparkle in her eyes.

"Veronica, it's Jacob. He has something he'd like to ask you."

I hope you enjoyed this snowy, locked-room mystery. The next Veronica Vale Investigates book is already available to order!

Death at the Fox and Fiddle.

A new year has arrived in the quiet London suburb of Hampstead, and The Fox and Fiddle Inn, owned by sleuth and journalist, Veronica Vale, is bustling with laughter, music, and village gossip. But the celebration turns tragic when barmaid Lillian Harrow is found dead in the pub's garden. With her sharp tongue and a habit of knowing everyone's secrets, Lillian made as many enemies as friends. And one of them just decided to silence her.

For Veronica, the murder is personal. The Fox and Fiddle was her late father's pride and joy. As whispers spread through the village and the police search for easy answers, Veronica and her loyal dog Benji dig deep into the lives of locals who would rather stay hidden.

Meanwhile, her dear friend Ruby is embracing motherhood with her new baby, Grace, but even happiness can't keep danger from creeping close to home. When another threat surfaces, Veronica must act fast to protect those she loves and uncover the truth before a killer strikes again.

Historical Note

The Thistle Inn: Although there are pubs named The Thistle Inn in Scotland (for example, there's one at Crossmichael, Dumfries & Galloway), there are no famous historic inns in the 1920s high society/estate context in this story. However, the name was so charming and such a perfect fit for the story, I embellished!

The evolution of Scottish castles: Many castles were originally built for defense, then used for residence, but by the 1920s, several estates and castles were changing due to economic realities. With the decline of landed wealth, some castles opened parts of their lands, grounds or residences for visitors, weddings, stays, and leisure pursuits.

Taymouth Castle, for example, was converted to a hydropathic hotel and a golf course in the mid-1920s.

Ornamental dirks: The Scottish dirk is well-documented as a traditional dagger, originally a weapon that evolved into a ceremonial accessory and became largely ceremonial or decorative, so it was no surprise to find two dirks displayed in a cabinet in the Thistle Inn.

Large wild animals: Keeping exotic wild animals really happened! There were menageries and exotic collections all over the country, and they were often a feature of the aristocracy and many country houses. This was a particular craze in the 18th and 19th centuries in the United Kingdom, including an estate that had wild Indian buffalo!

About the author

Immerse yourself into Kitty Kildare's cleverly woven historical British mysteries. Follow the mystery in the Veronica Vale Investigates series and enjoy the dazzle and delights of 1920s England.

Kitty is a not-so-secret pen name of established cozy mystery author K.E.O'Connor, who decided she wanted to time travel rather than cast spells! Enjoy the twists and turns.

Join in the fun and get Kitty's newsletter (and secret wartime files about our sleuthing ladies!)

Newsletter: https://BookHip.com/JJPKDLB
Website: www.kittykildare.com
Facebook: www.facebook.com/kittykildare

www.ingramcontent.com/pod-product-compliance
Lightning Source LLC
Chambersburg PA
CDIIW050610190726
48283CB00007B/2361